Laura turned and glared, the loveliness on her face gone.

"I assume you have something else to wear other than a tuxedo? We'll be doing real work today, Mr. Holbrook. This won't be a party."

Her attitude irked Adam. He started to say something smart, but remembered Mr. Durrant's request for respect. Something she'd said suddenly clicked into place. "We?"

Laura Durrant placed her hands on her hips and took a step toward him. "We. You'll be under my supervision for the duration of your sentence. I'll be showing you how to rebuild what you destroyed, and I want to get started today if that's all right with you."

Adam looked over her head to her father. There was a knowing and sympathetic smile on his face. He shrugged.

"My daughter is a skilled carpenter and contractor. Trust me, she knows her stuff." He took his daughter's arm and tugged her along with him out of the room. "We'll leave you alone to get ready. Don't take too long."

Books by Lorraine Beatty

Love Inspired

Rekindled Romance
Restoring His Heart

LORRAINE BEATTY

was born and raised in Columbus, Ohio, but has been
blessed to live in Germany, Connecticut and Baton
Rouge. She now calls Mississippi home. She and her
husband, Joe, have two sons and six grandchildren.
Lorraine started writing in junior high and has written
for trade books, newspapers and company newslet-
ters. She is a member of RWA and ACFW and is a
charter member and past president of Magnolia State
Romance Writers. In her spare time she likes to work
in her garden, travel and spend time with her family.

Restoring His Heart

Lorraine Beatty

DISCARD

Recycling programs for this product may not exist in your area.

™ LOVE INSPIRED BOOKS

ISBN-13: 978-0-373-87821-5

RESTORING HIS HEART

www.LoveInspiredBooks.com

Printed in U.S.A.

Give, and it will be given to you. A good measure, pressed down, shaken together and running over, will be poured into your lap. For with the same measure you use, it will be measured to you.

—*Luke* 6:38

To my sweet hubby, Joe, who is always there cheering me on and offering hugs. I love you. And to Melissa for her help, her guidance and mostly her patience. I couldn't have done it without you.

Chapter One

Adam Holbrook stood and faced the bench of the Honorable Judge Hankins A. Wallace. The man seated there didn't look anything like what he'd expected. He'd envisioned the judge in a small rural town like Dover, Mississippi, to be a balding, overweight, quirky character with horn-rimmed glasses perched on the end of his nose. One look at this magistrate had given Adam his first moment of concern.

Judge Wallace was stern-faced and imposing, and it had nothing to do with his being elevated behind the bench. Broad shoulders, steely brown eyes and a set to his jaw that made it clear he was in charge. Adam's throat went dry. He glanced over at his court-appointed attorney. He'd considered calling his own attorney yesterday after he'd been arrested for reckless endangerment and destroying public property, a result of his accidently running his car into the town's park and damaging a small building. But his attorney was also his most recent girlfriend and the relationship had ended badly, so he'd chosen to go with a court-appointed lawyer. Now he questioned that decision.

"Adam Holbrook?"

"Yes, Your Honor." He put as much respect and sincerity into his tone as possible.

"Were you driving drunk in my town, Mr. Holbrook?"

"No, sir."

The judge's dark gaze pierced him from across the room. "So, then what were you doing when you decided to destroy our beloved landmark?"

He opened his mouth to protest, then changed his mind. Better to eat crow and be on his way. In twenty-eight days he had to be seated at the board of directors meeting of his father's company, Holbrook Electronics, or lose the yearly allowance from his trust fund forever. There were no excuses acceptable. Either be in Atlanta on time or face financial ruin. "I was trying to use the GPS on my phone."

The judge nodded knowingly and glanced at the papers on his desk. "Uh-huh. Well then, let's get straight to it. I'm sure you're anxious to get this over with."

Adam allowed a small grin. "As a matter of fact I am. I have interests in Atlanta that require my immediate attention." He was pleased with his calm, respectful tone. Hope rose. All he had to do now was meet the bail, pay any fines and he could be on his way.

"Do you now?" Judge Wallace took the folder in front of him in his hands and scanned the contents. "It says here you're some kind of minor celebrity. That you like to indulge in all manner of extreme sporting adventures." His tone was thick with disapproval.

Hope took a nosedive. He might have grossly underestimated this small town's justice system. He waited, a heightened sense of anticipation sparking his nerves, similar to the sensation he experienced right before he jumped out of a plane or dived off a cliff.

The judge leaned back in his chair, frowning. "We do things a bit differently here in Dover, Mr. Holbrook. We believe in the punishment fitting the crime."

"I'll be more than happy to have the structure repaired, Your Honor." That should score a few points.

"That's good to hear. That's what I had in mind, as well. You see, that wasn't any old structure you crashed your flashy silver car into. That was an historic landmark. It's the symbol of this town. It's one hundred and thirty years old and we're rather fond of that gazebo."

A small bead of sweat trickled down his back. "Yes, sir."

"So, here's what you're going to do." The judge straightened in his chair and banged his gavel on the bench. "You're hereby sentenced to thirty days under house arrest. And you will spend those days rebuilding the gazebo you damaged. Any spare hours will be spent doing community service."

Adam struggled to grasp what the judge had just said. He couldn't be serious. "Your Honor, I have urgent personal matters in Atlanta that require my presence."

The judge shook his head. "That's unfortunate. Thirty days."

No. Thirty days would mean he'd miss the deadline. There were no contingencies with the rules of his trust fund. No leeway. He either showed up for the meeting or he was cut off. Permanently. Once Arthur Holbrook made a decree it was carved in stone. Especially something like this. "Your Honor, what about bail? I'm able to meet any amount you deem equitable."

"Yes, I'm sure you're more than able. That's the

point, Mr. Holbrook. I suspect buying your way out of things is a bad habit with you. No bail."

"Your Honor…"

The judge held up his hand. "I figure that gazebo damage is well within the felony limits. You're fortunate that no one was injured in your little stunt or you could be facing manslaughter charges."

Dryness in his throat made it hard to swallow. He had been greatly relieved that no one had been injured, but he couldn't afford to be stuck in rural Mississippi for a month. He searched frantically for a way out of this mess. He looked to his attorney, who shrugged and shook his head. He was on his own. A surge of anger rushed through his veins. What else was new? Adam faced the bench again. He flashed his most engaging smile. "With all due respect, sir, I don't know how to repair that building."

"I suspect not. That's why I'm assigning an expert to help you out. And because you're such an unusual case, you'll be housed with a local family instead of the jail, and you'll be wearing an ankle monitor at all times until you've completed your sentence."

The tone of the judge's voice and the look in his eyes told Adam there was no point in trying to press his case. He'd have to find some other way to get home in time. Missing the yearly meeting with his father was out of the question. He had to be in Atlanta on time or lose everything.

Laura Durrant shut the tailgate on her truck and walked to the cab, pulling herself up into the driver's seat. She'd stopped by her workshop to pick up the tools she would need to get everything secured at the gazebo.

Her heart ached when she thought about the damage the accident had caused. Some daredevil rich guy had lost control of his sports car and driven through the fence surrounding the courthouse square and rammed into their historic gazebo. Now it was up to her to fix it.

As a licensed contractor and builder, her company, LC Construction, specialized in restoring old homes and buildings. Her job was physically and mentally stressful, but she loved every second of it. At least she usually did. At the moment she had more work than she could handle and more problems, too.

She was still kicking herself for agreeing to this project. Her uncle, Judge Wallace, was fond of sentencing those who passed through his court to unusual punishments. Normally she applauded the idea, but this was the first time the punishment had included her. When her uncle had requested her help, she'd been eager to repair the gazebo. No one would do it more lovingly or more accurately than she would.

What she disliked was having to work with Adam Holbrook for the next thirty days. She didn't have time to rehabilitate some spoiled rich guy who had nothing better to do than tool around the country in his vintage sports car. He would only get in the way and slow things down. Unfortunately, she had no choice. But she would make sure he pulled his weight.

One thing she knew for certain. The gazebo would be restored in time for the Founder's Day Festival, Dover's most important event of the year. She'd do whatever it took to make sure that happened.

Adam followed Officer Don Barnes down the hallway, the weight of his newly attached ankle tracking device a grim reminder of his fate. He'd been processed for his house arrest. Now he was being taken to meet his jailers.

Once seated in the back of the patrol car, Adam tried to think of some way out of his predicament. He touched the bandage on his jaw where it had hit the steering wheel when he crashed. He'd been lucky. No major injuries. A scraped jaw, a bruised shoulder and a seriously wounded ego were all he'd suffered. He'd gotten off better than the little gazebo had. He glanced down at his once-elegant silk shirt and the dirt marring his tuxedo pants. He probably should have changed when he left the party in Dallas yesterday morning, but he'd been anxious to get his newly purchased '63 Porsche 356 out on the open highway. He sighed, letting his gaze drift to his feet. He tugged up his pant leg and looked at the ugly black monitor. He was trapped. In a prison without bars.

Turning his attention to the scenery outside the vehicle, he shook his head with bewilderment. The streets along the town square were lined with what most people would see as charming old buildings and an even more charming old courthouse. To him they were just old, out-of-date and dull.

He liked things big and wide open. Dangerous. Risky. For fifty-one weeks a year he was his own man. He went where he wanted and did what he wanted. He'd surfed the big waves in Waimea, heli-skiied in British Columbia and raced a car at Daytona. He lived a life of danger and excitement other men only dreamed of.

At least he used to. Lately, he'd been finding it harder and harder to catch that high. The adrenaline rush wasn't coming as quickly, and the satisfaction from each thrill was missing. He'd been restless and irritable for over a year now and he could find no explanation for the sudden change.

The cruiser pulled to a stop in front of a large two-story white house on the corner that resembled something from a Norman Rockwell painting. Tall columns braced the wide porch. Broad front steps were decorated with pumpkins and fall flowers. Maybe this was a bed and breakfast. He could handle that.

The officer got out of the car at the same moment a man emerged from the house. He stopped at the edge of the porch steps and waited. When the officer opened the rear door, Adam got out, making a quick scan of the neighborhood. The street was lined with giant trees, the stately homes positioned in manicured lawns. Maybe staying with this family wouldn't be so bad after all. Still, he didn't like the idea of being watched over by strangers like some errant teenager.

He glanced up at the man on the porch. His stern expression said it all. He'd tolerate no nonsense in his home. Adam hid the smirk that fought to emerge. Just like his dad. My way or the highway. It was beginning to look like a very long thirty days ahead.

"Don, how's it going today?"

The officer kept a firm hold on Adam's upper arm as he led him to the foot of the steps. At least he'd been spared the handcuffs. "Doing good. I brought your houseguest." He turned to Adam, a disapproving scowl on his narrow face. "Mr. Holbrook, meet your jailer, Mr. Durrant. This here is Adam Holbrook." Without waiting for either man to speak, the officer released Adam and placed his hands on his hips. "His ankle monitor is set for one mile. If LC needs more range, just have her call and we'll adjust it. You need me to go over anything before I go?"

"No, Don. Hank and I worked it all out. Thanks. I have it from here."

The officer offered a small salute and walked off. Adam squared his shoulders and faced the man. Whatever it was, he would endure. He'd jumped out of helicopters. Surviving a month in a small town should be a piece of cake.

The man came closer toward him, a warm smile on his face. Adam's guard went up. What kind of people would welcome a prisoner into their home?

"I guess Don was in a hurry to get back to work. I'm Tom Durrant. Welcome to our home, Mr. Holbrook." He held out his hand.

Adam grasped it, surprised to find the hand strong and calloused. It didn't fit with the stately old home. Adam had always been good at knowing when someone was conning him. Something was going on here.

Durrant turned and went back up the steps, motioning for Adam to follow. Mr. Durrant looked to be late fifties, early sixties. Tall, broad-shouldered, with silver-gray hair, his quick movements spoke of a man in good shape physically. So what was the catch?

Inside the house, Mr. Durrant stopped in the foyer and waited for him to enter, that same pleasant smile on his face. "I know you're anxious to get settled, but I think we need to have a little talk first. Are you hungry? Did you get breakfast this morning?"

"No, sir." Adam followed him into a bright sunny kitchen at the back of the house. The room was large with a round table positioned in a cozy corner filled with windows.

"I thought not. Have a seat and I'll get you fixed up. Coffee?"

He nodded, growing more confused by the moment. Was this where he'd stay? What was going on? Were they trying to kill him with kindness for damaging the little gazebo in the square? Cruel and unusual punishment for sure.

Adam sat down, realizing how out of place he looked in his bedraggled tuxedo. This kitchen was more suited to the jeans and polo shirt his jailer was wearing. Mr. Durrant returned to the table with a plate of cinnamon rolls and a steaming cup of coffee, which made Adam's stomach growl. He'd barely touched his food since being arrested yesterday.

"Here ya go. Eat up. Those rolls were homemade this morning by my wife. She's a great cook."

Adam eyed the man suspiciously. "Thanks." Mr. Durrant waited while Adam doctored his coffee with a little cream and sugar and took a roll from the plate.

"I imagine you have some questions. Let me go over the high points and then I'll show you to your room. Number one, this will be your home for the duration of your sentence. You will be allowed to wander anywhere on our property, but nowhere else. Check-in is whenever you stop work for the day, and you're required to call the police station within five minutes of your arrival here. You'll be picked up for work each day and brought home each night. Oh, and only one phone call per day."

He pulled a cell from his shirt pocket that Adam instantly recognized as his own. He started to reach for it. Mr. Durrant shook his head.

"Sorry. I know how you young people live and die by these things, but we'll keep it down here on that table over there. You can make your calls in here." He smiled. "Don't worry, we'll give you all the privacy you need."

Adam swallowed a bite of cinnamon roll. It was the best he'd ever tasted, but he wasn't in the mood to truly enjoy it. "Is that all?"

Clasping his hands on the table, Mr. Durrant leaned toward him. "Treat my wife and me with respect, behave yourself and everything should be fine. Any other questions?"

Adam set his coffee cup down with a firm thud. "Why are you doing this? It doesn't make sense."

Tom Durrant smiled again. "You'll understand soon enough. But I will tell you that the judge is my brother-in-law. Apparently you're something of a celebrity and he thought you'd be better off here with us than being locked up in the county jail. Because you'll be working on the gazebo, this was a logical place to put you. And—" Mr. Durrant inhaled a deep breath "—I have a personal stake in the matter."

Adam was beginning to wish they'd locked him up in a nice safe cell with ordinary criminals. He was used to dealing with people who wanted something from him. But this was different. He didn't like being off balance, and this situation had him teetering like a tightrope walker over a canyon.

"Well, you'll be going to work soon, so we'd better get you settled in."

Adam followed Tom Durrant through the large home. And it was a home. A place where people lived. Signs of life were on display everywhere. Magnets held scribbled drawings on the refrigerator door. An open book lay upside down on an end table. A sweater draped over a chair. The furniture was traditional and tasteful, but comfortably used. A pile of magazines lay on the stairs as if waiting to be taken up. Family photos covered the wall along the stairway. Too many for him to process as they passed by. He'd never seen pictures displayed like this. The only picture in his home growing up was the portrait of his mother in her favorite ball gown which hung over the fireplace in the main salon.

Upstairs, Tom Durrant led him to a room at the far end of the hall. Adam stepped inside, his attention falling on the items on the bed. "My bags." He walked to the bed, quickly sliding open the zipper on the small case. The sight of his personal items filled him with a rush of comfort.

"They sent your things over this morning. I knew you'd need some different clothes to work in. Carpentry is dirty work." He walked across the room and opened another door, flipping on the switch to reveal a private bathroom. "I think you'll find everything you need. If not, just ask and we'll see what we can do." He smiled again. "Within reason of course."

A sudden lump of gratitude rose in Adam's chest. While he still harbored serious doubts about this arrangement, at least he'd have a place to retreat to each night, a place to be alone. And alone was where he was most comfortable. "Thanks. This will be fine."

"Daddy!"

Adam turned at the sound of the female voice.

"Up here, Boo."

Adam waited as the sound of pounding footsteps rumbled on the steps and along the hall. From the noise being made, he expected someone large and sturdy to appear in the doorway. He wasn't prepared for the woman who stepped into the room.

"Hey, Daddy."

She was short, five foot four tops. At first glance he thought she was a teenager, but on closer inspection he realized she was probably not much younger than himself. Perhaps thirty-one or thirty-two.

"You're putting him in Matt's room? I thought you'd put him in the spare room over the garage."

Tom Durrant shook his head. "Too isolated up there. I thought it would be better if he was close by."

Adam didn't like the sound of that. Was Mr. Durrant going to monitor him every moment?

"Mr. Holbrook, this is my daughter, Laura Durrant."

She made no move to shake his hand, so he merely nodded. From the scowl on her face, he had a feeling she was not going to be one of his fans. She turned to look at her father and Adam felt a small skip in his heartbeat when her features suddenly changed from disapproving to near worshipful. The love in her eyes for her father gave her a glow.

"We need to get going. How soon will he be ready?"

"Ask him."

She turned and glared, the loveliness on her face gone. "I assume you have something else to wear other than a tuxedo? We'll be doing real work today, Mr. Holbrook. This won't be a party."

Her attitude irked him. He started to say something smart, but remembered Mr. Durrant's request for respect. Something she'd said suddenly clicked into place. "We?"

Laura Durrant placed her hands on her hips and took a step toward him. "We. You'll be under my supervision for the duration of your sentence. I'll be showing you how to rebuild what you destroyed, and I want to get started today if that's all right with you."

Adam looked over her head to her father. There was a knowing and sympathetic smile on his face. He shrugged.

"My daughter is a skilled carpenter and contractor. Trust me, she knows her stuff." He took his daughter's arm and tugged her along with him out of the room. "We'll leave you alone to get ready. Don't take too long. She gets cranky when she has to wait."

"Dad."

The door shut behind them, but not before Adam heard Tom Durrant gently scold "Boo" for her attitude.

Adam dragged a hand across his face. Surely this had to be some kind of bizarre parallel universe. No way could he take orders from that little slip of a thing. He had to find a way out of this mess. And fast.

Laura followed her father downstairs to the kitchen. "He'd better not take all day primping. I want to get started on that gazebo today. I've got too many other things I need to take care of." Her dad pointed to a kitchen chair.

"Sit. I'm sure he'll be down directly. How's the Mobile situation?"

Laura sat down, resting her head dejectedly on one palm. Her last restoration project had been in Mobile, Alabama, on a historic downtown building. Unfortunately, the owner had suddenly declared bankruptcy and everything was on hold. Including her pay. "Awful. The lawyers are going to draw this thing out as long as possible so they don't have to pay up."

"What does your attorney say?"

"He's doing all he can, but you know the court system works like molasses." She exhaled and leaned back in her chair. "I never would have taken that job if I'd known the company would go belly-up a week after I completed the work."

Her dad chuckled. "We all wish we had a crystal ball to see into the future, but that's not how the good Lord set things up. We're supposed to rely on Him, not ourselves. You upheld your part of the deal. That's all you can do."

"I know, but in the meantime, I have payroll to meet. That job was going to give me enough financial security to breathe easy for the next year. And then there's the Keller building." She looked over at her father, wishing he could make it all better the way he had when she was small. But at thirty-two, her troubles were her own to battle.

Her dad laid his hand on top of hers. "I wish I could help you somehow. Your mom and I have been talking to everyone we know looking for people who would be interested in stepping up to save the old place, but no luck."

"I know. Money is tight everywhere. I don't blame anyone, but it's so frustrating. If I could only have convinced Mr. Keller to sell me the building or get it listed on the Historic Registry before he died. Now it's going up for auction in a few weeks and I've run out of options. Buying it myself was the only one left and now that's off the table, too. Without the profits from the Mobile job I can't afford to even bid on it."

The old three-story building at the corner of Main and Peace streets downtown would make a perfect senior center once it was restored. Something she'd wanted to do for a long time. The center would provide a safe place for seniors to meet and do their crafts. It would also be a place where they could teach others the numerous skills they possessed. Crocheting. Knitting. Tole painting. Sewing. Quilting. She hated seeing the old building falling apart when it could be brought to life again and made useful. It was structurally sound and perfectly located. All it needed was some work. Okay, a lot of work, but work she was more than willing to do.

Laura stood and walked to the door leading to the hallway. "What's taking him so long?"

"Give him time, Boo. He'll be down soon enough."

"And that's another thing. I've got the Conrad job going on. My foreman keeps running into problems every time we open a wall or rip up a floorboard. I don't have time to spend repairing what this poor little rich boy did. And there's only a few weeks to restore the gazebo in time for the Founder's Day Festival. That doesn't give me much leeway for finding materials. Dealing with him will double the time needed to make repairs. Not to mention the mistakes that will have to be undone and the wasted lumber from incorrect measurements."

"I can speak to your uncle Hank. He could find someone else to restore the gazebo," her father said.

Laura whirled around. "No, I want to do it. I just wish I had someone competent to help me. Not an amateur." She puffed out her irritation and paced the room.

"Maybe he'll surprise you and be a quick study, or maybe he already has a few skills that will be helpful." Her dad came and gave her a hug. "It'll all work out, Boo. Have a little faith."

Laura smiled at her dad. She hoped he was right this time. "So, what do you think of him?"

"Hard to say. I've only spoken to him briefly. I think he's unhappy with his situation, but that's understandable. He reminds me of your brother Ty. As I recall, you had no trouble keeping him in line."

She smiled. "So you're saying I can take him?"

"No doubt, but don't get carried away. Something tells me this man has a thick wall of protection around him. With Ty you always knew where he stood. He didn't keep his feelings hidden. I suspect Adam has kept his feelings buried most of his life. Don't be too hard on him." He turned and picked up his cell phone and slipped it in his pocket. "Time to get to the store. Your mother will be wondering where I am."

"You're leaving me here alone with this stranger?"

"I don't think you're in any danger. That's one of the reasons your mom and I agreed to let him stay here. I wanted to make sure he understood that you're my baby girl and he'd better watch his p's and q's." He chuckled and started for the door. "Maybe I should have warned him about you. You're tougher than both your brothers put together."

Laura waved goodbye to her dad, then checked her watch again. She'd lost nearly half an hour waiting for Mr. Rich Adventurer. If he wasn't down in ten minutes, she'd go in and drag his spoiled self out by the scruff of his neck.

She had to admit, she'd been surprised at her first glimpse of him. She tried to ignore the way his startling green eyes had made a swift but thorough assessment of her. Doubtful she could compare with the kind of women he was used to. And she felt sure he was used to taking his pick of leggy beauties.

She couldn't blame her fellow females for falling for this guy. He had all the right stuff on the outside. His six-foot frame and thick light brown hair made him boyishly handsome.

But she preferred a man of faith. A man with character in his face and compassion in his heart.

Heavy footsteps on the stairs let her know Holbrook was finally ready. He stepped through the kitchen door and stopped, his green gaze slamming into hers. Her throat closed up and her heart skipped a couple beats. A short while ago he'd resembled James Bond fresh from saving the world. Now, he stood in the kitchen looking ready for a photo shoot for a Rugged Men of the South calendar. The gray knit Henley shirt hugged his chest and broad shoulders like an old friend and brought out the vibrant green of his eyes. The jeans called attention to his narrow waist and long powerful legs. A pair of well-worn dark boots anchored him to the floor. Apparently, adventurers needed sturdy footwear in their wardrobes.

She shook her head, trying to regain her composure. "If you're ready, we need to get going."

There was a half smile on his face. "Ready as I'll ever be."

Laura pushed through the back door and headed for her red truck. "I hope you're ready to work because we have a lot to do and very little time to get it done."

Chapter Two

Adam followed Laura Durrant to her truck and climbed in, wondering how so small a woman could command such authority. Her no-nonsense attitude was intriguing and a bit intimidating. He'd decided to be a good scout, do what he was told and get the lay of the land. Eventually he'd find a loophole, some way to get out of Dover and back to Atlanta on time. Of course there was always his last resort—calling one of his dad's lawyers. He didn't want to think about the repercussions of that.

He glanced over at Laura Durrant. Her slender figure was obscured by stained and faded jeans, ending in heavy brown work boots. That explained the loud thumping on the stairs. Her purple T-shirt was worn and faded, with a quarter-sized hole in one sleeve. Her head was covered with a ball cap and spikes of hair stuck out from the adjustment opening in the back and the edges over her ears. He guessed at its color. Dishwater blond? What stood out the most were her violet blue eyes. Eyes that were staring at him with disdain. She looked small behind the wheel of the big truck but absolutely in control. Which raised a lot of questions. "So, you're in charge of the work detail, huh?"

"That's right. You answer to me."

"What do I call you?"

"You can call me Boss or LC."

"I thought your name was Boo." He saw her scowl at the name.

"My dad is the only one who calls me that. And my brother Ty sometimes. LC is the name of the company. LC Construction and Restoration."

Adam wanted to ask what the initials stood for, but decided it might be safer to wait on that. "So how long do you think this repair job will take? How much damage did I do?"

She glanced at him briefly, eyes narrowed. "It's not a repair job, Mr. Holbrook. It's a restoration and that takes a lot more time."

"Restoration. Repair. Same difference, isn't it?"

"Not even close. The building you drove your little car into is a National Historic Landmark. Which is why I'm doing the job. If all it needed was repairing, any competent carpenter could do the work in a few days."

"And what makes you different?"

"I'm a certified restorationist."

"Meaning?"

"I'm qualified to restore old homes and buildings to their original state when possible. That's what I do."

"I didn't know there was such a thing. How did you get to be one?" She exhaled an exasperated sigh as if reluctant to explain.

"I studied architecture in college, but I found I didn't like the designing as much as I liked the hands-on ground-level work. When I moved home, I bought this construction company from a local man who was retiring. He did a lot of restoration work, so all I had to do was expand on that customer base."

"Still, a girl in construction. Where did that come from?"

Laura turned and smiled, her expression softening the way it had when she'd looked at her father earlier. Something inside Adam shifted.

"Oh. My dad owns the hardware store in town. I grew up around nuts and bolts."

She turned back to the road ahead. "So how did you come to lose control of your car and ram it into our historic gazebo?"

For a moment Adam considered avoiding the question, but then he remembered her uncle was the judge and her father his jailer. No point in trying to hide the truth. "I left a friend's house in Dallas early yesterday morning and planned on spending a few days in New Orleans. You know, eating fine food, listening to good music, maybe do a little deep-sea fishing. I got hungry, saw a billboard for some mom-and-pop diner in Sawyers Bend—"

"Jingles."

"What?"

"The name of the diner is Jingles."

"Right. Well, somehow I missed the turnoff and ended up in your fair community. I was trying to find a way back to the interstate on my smartphone and the rest you know."

"You didn't have GPS in that fancy car of yours?"

"No, it's a vintage machine. I was going to have it installed after my meeting in Atlanta."

Laura Durrant pulled the truck to a stop along the

fence line near the gazebo. "Too bad you didn't have that done before you left Dallas. Might have saved everyone a lot of trouble."

Adam scanned the area. Yellow police tape marked the site. His car had been removed and he could clearly see the gaping hole in the side of the little building. He climbed out of the cab and joined the boss lady at the back of her truck. "Where do you suppose my car is?"

"I have no idea. Impound probably. You won't be needing it for a while."

"No, but I'd like to see about having it repaired. I'll have to leave here eventually." He took the hard hat and work gloves she handed him. He tucked the gloves in the back pocket of his jeans and tried the hat on for size, pulling it off again and adjusting the band inside.

LC broke the caution tape and walked toward the damaged section of the gazebo.

"Should you be crossing that police line?"

"We'll put up our own safety fencing."

Up close, Adam was surprised to find the gazebo larger than he'd expected. He figured it was about twenty-four feet across. He also had a clearer picture of the damage he'd caused and he wondered if anything could be salvaged. He saw tire tracks in the dirt where he'd tried to stop, and pieces of glass were scattered around the ground from his broken windshield. A gaping hole in the brick foundation of the gazebo marked the spot where his car had come to rest. He looked upward at the roof which sagged from the loss of several broken support beams. The cupola on top tilted at a precarious angle and the decorative spindles were little more than kindling.

He glanced over at Laura, stunned to see a deep sadness in her eyes. For a moment he thought she might burst into tears. Did the old gazebo mean that much to her? He didn't understand. It was just a small building in the center of the town.

But the sadness in her eyes made him so uncomfortable that he looked away, scanning the area. Surely the workers would show up anytime now. He was anxious to meet the real carpenters. She may own the construction company, but a woman her size couldn't lift a can of paint by herself, let alone a two-by-four. He could, however, see her as the boss. With her hardline attitude and biting comments, he doubted any man would dare to cross her. "So when do the others arrive?"

"What others?"

"The carpenters and guys with the muscle."

"Sorry, Holbrook, no others. Just you and me. My guys are all busy on other jobs. I can't afford to pull them off to do this restoration."

Adam frowned. "I wasn't expecting it would be just the two of us."

"I'm sure there's going to be a lot of things you aren't expecting."

He stared at the small structure, rubbing his jaw. "You sure we can't use more help?"

"It's not that big a deal. We'll do the woodworking and I'll sub out the other trades." He drew his eyebrows together. "I employ four full-time carpenters, one fabricator and a cabinet maker. The rest of the work is hired out to subcontractors. Like the brick work, electrical and drywall and tile. The mill will build the post and spindles. Any other craftsmen I need I'll hire to do the work."

Adam nodded in understanding and followed her

to the damaged corner, watching as she stooped down and inspected the gaping hole in the brick foundation. She pulled out one crumbling brick and examined it, a look of disgust on her face. She stood and held up the partially destroyed pale red brick.

"Do you have any idea how hard it's going to be to find more of these?"

He grinned. "Can't we run over to the local brickyard?"

She tossed the brick on the ground and glared. "That gazebo is over one hundred and thirty years old. Those bricks are handmade. I can't walk into a store and buy more like you can replace that little car of yours."

"That car was built in the 1960s. It's worth ten times your little house."

"House?" Laura set her jaw, eyes blazing.

"It's a gazebo. It's old. I'll give you the money to build one twice that size with all the bells and whistles."

She crossed her arms over her chest. "First, we don't want a bigger, better gazebo, we want this one. It's a historic landmark. Second, I know you have no idea what you've done to this town or the history that you've destroyed, but believe me, it's significant. Third, I'm sure paying for everything is your usual method of getting out of trouble. Well, not this time. You're going to help me rebuild this and I can't wait to see you sweat and break your back doing it." She stomped off. Adam watched her go, tempted to walk out of this small insignificant town. Then he remembered the ankle bracelet.

He wouldn't get far.

Laura worked off her irritation by pulling out the orange plastic safety fencing and the stakes to anchor it from the truck bed. She had to regain her sense of control or she'd end up with a helper who might go AWOL on her. As much as she hated to face it, she would need his upper-body strength to wield some of the beams and timbers she'd need to rebuild things. She started back toward the gazebo, her heart tightening at the sight of the wounded structure. Adam came toward her, arms extended.

"I'll get those." He took the cumbersome material from her grasp. "Where do you want them?"

"I want you to set up a perimeter about twelve to sixteen feet from the gazebo to give us room to work and set up the equipment we'll need. Be sure to leave an opening so we can come and go. You'll find a special fencepost driver tool in the back of the truck. It's red and looks like a pipe with handles. Use that to set the posts about eight feet apart." Adam started to move off, then turned back.

"You want exact spacing or approximate?"

"Approximate will do. I just don't want people getting too close while we work." Laura stapled the building permit encased in protective plastic to one post, leaving Adam to figure the mechanics of the fencing. Retrieving her electronic tablet from the truck, she started her detailed list of the materials she'd need and the specifications for the gazebo to start tracking down the lumber from the correct era.

She glanced at Adam smiling as he tugged the flimsy orange fencing between the posts. She let him struggle for a while, intending to give him some pointers, but the next time she looked, he'd gotten the hang of it. He finished his task at the same time she completed her list.

"How did I do, boss?"

The grin on his face made his eyes sparkle. "Fine. You'll have to check it each day. It tends to sag over time."

"What's next? Power tools?"

"No. We have to stabilize the roof, then take all this damaged section apart." She picked up a pair of protective goggles. "But first we need to go over a few safety rules. You will wear these when using power tools, and earplugs when running the saw. Use a waist support when we do heavy lifting and never, I repeat, never treat a power tool with anything less than the utmost respect. They aren't toys."

Adam nodded. "I might not understand the tools, but I do know a thing or two about safety and being cautious. I make sure my sports equipment is thoroughly checked out before I use it. I don't take unnecessary risks."

Laura huffed under her breath. "Yet you still risk your life for nothing more than a temporary thrill." She turned and motioned for him to follow. "We need to support the roof before we do anything else. I'll get the jack, you bring that four-by-six post over here."

Laura positioned the jack in the center of the gazebo and instructed Adam how to position the heavy post to take the weight of the roof. She'd anticipated his resistance today, but so far he'd followed her every command without question. She held the post in place while Adam put his strength behind the jack, pumping the handle. She glanced down at him, surprised to see him watching the upward movement of the beam closely as he worked. She also was suddenly aware of the muscles in his arms and the way the fabric of his shirt strained across his shoulders as he moved.

"Is that enough?"

Laura jerked her attention back to the beam. It was touching under the center of the roof but not firmly enough. "Another inch should do it." Satisfied, she stepped back, watching as Adam rose to his full height and placed his hand on the beam.

"Will this one piece of wood hold up this whole building?"

She swallowed and took a step back. "It's only a temporary fix until we can assess the damage to the rafters and make the repairs."

"Okay." He smiled. "What's next?"

Laura searched her mind for the next task she wanted him to do, but her thoughts were muddled with things she rarely thought about. Like how strong Adam was, and how small she felt beside him. He made her aware that she was very female and he was so male. She forced herself to focus on the work. "We need to start stacking the loose bricks over there out of the way. We'll reuse the ones that aren't too damaged. Make a pallet out of scrap lumber and stack them on that. It'll keep them from sinking into the ground. I need to make some phone calls."

Without waiting for his response, she walked to her truck and climbed inside. She needed time to think and space away from Adam Holbrook. He reminded her a little too much of her ex-husband, Ted—concerned with his own life with never a thought to anyone else and no appreciation for anything of value. She closed her eyes and offered up a prayer for tolerance and forgiveness. It didn't matter what Holbrook was like. All she needed was for him to help her get the gazebo restored in time for the festival and then he could go on about his merry way.

Adam pried the last loose brick from the foundation and stacked it with the others. He was hot, sweaty and his back ached. He had no idea dismantling the little building would be such hard work. He wasn't quite sure what to make of his new boss. It was obvious she loved what she did. To him, the debris looked like so much broken wood. To her, each piece was a special hand-crafted treasure.

Adam leaned against the side of the gazebo, wiping his forehead with his sleeve. Reaching down, he took a bottle of water from the small cooler she kept nearby. His gaze traveled around the square inventorying the rows of businesses. The usual stuff. Couple of banks. A diner. Pizza place. Antique shop. Drug store. Hardware store. Her daddy's store? He smiled. Daddy could keep an eye on his little girl all day long from his store. Interesting. The damaged gazebo. A daughter in construction. A father willing to help out to keep her safe. Normally he would scoff at such behavior, but having met her father, and her, he could hardly blame Tom Durrant for wanting to keep watch. He found it a bit old-fashioned but sweet.

Laura had made it clear she thought he was incapable of doing anything without assistance. He was looking forward to proving her wrong. How hard could swinging a hammer be? He finished his water and tossed it into the trash can just outside the orange fence.

Laura came toward him from the truck, slipping her cell phone into the small holster on her hip. "Okay, I found brick down in Long Beach, left over from a Katrina salvage. They're shipping it up. Should be here by Tuesday."

She stared at him expectantly, as if he should grasp the significance of her words. The excitement in her expression lit up her violet blue eyes. He'd never seen a color like that before. Nor had he realized how the hard hat made her features appear delicate and fragile. But Adam knew better. There was nothing fragile about this lady. He blinked. She was waiting for some reaction from him. "Is that good?"

"More than good. But replacing that foundation will take time."

"Is time a big deal?"

"Yes, it is. We're having our annual Founder's Day Festival at the end of the month and this 'little house' is the centerpiece. If this gazebo is unusable for the festival it'll be like Christmas without a tree. It's *that* important." She sighed and pulled on her gloves. "I don't expect you to understand."

He watched her out of the corner of his eye, captivated by her passion for the little structure. Her eyes flashed like a summer storm, her cheeks flushed, turning her violet eyes to deep purple. He forced his mind back to the job at hand. "What now, boss?"

She pointed to the broken railing. "Start pulling that apart and stack it over there. Keep all the like pieces together. We'll have to use them as templates later. Don't throw anything away unless I okay it."

"So you're going to recycle all this? Saving the planet and all that?"

"In a way. All this lumber is original. I want to keep as much of it as possible not only for the historic value, but to keep the historic designation, too. The structure has to be comprised of a certain percentage of original materials to be on the registry."

Adam worked a spindle loose from the splintered floor board. His gaze drifted toward Laura again. She moved like a little dynamo, never still. Even when she was on the phone, which was frequently, she paced. He'd seen her sitting on the tailgate of the truck once when she was studying her tablet, but she hadn't sat there long. It was easy to see why her business was a success. She worked hard and with passion.

"Good morning."

Adam turned and looked over his shoulder. A man a few years older than he was standing near the orange fencing, a warm, friendly smile on his face. He studied the gazebo intently, while slipping his hands into the pockets of his jeans. Adam braced himself for some nasty comments. Several locals had drifted past this morning, but all they'd done was scowl. Sooner or later he'd known the words would start to fly.

The man nodded toward him. "You the man responsible for this damage?"

Adam stood and faced the man. "I am."

The man's smile widened. "It's nice to meet an honest and forthright man." He stepped forward and extended his hand. "Jim Barrett. You must be Adam Holbrook."

The man's handshake was firm and steady, his smile and friendly tone took any condemnation out of the words. "I seem to have acquired a reputation overnight. Literally."

"So you have. But because you're working to make things right, the good folks of Dover will forgive you soon enough. Provided it's finished in time for the big festival."

"Jim, what are you up to today?" Laura walked past Adam to the fence, opening her arms to the man for a quick hug. Apparently they were close friends.

"I just got back from rounds at the hospital and thought I'd come by and see how things are going here." He glanced over at Adam. "Mr. Holbrook looks like he will be a competent assistant for you."

Laura looked askance at Adam. "He might make a good saw boy eventually. We'll see." She turned to Adam. "Jim is the associate pastor at our church."

Adam took another look at the man. He guessed him to be in his late thirties. He had kind eyes and a gentle manner. He could easily see this man leading a flock of believers, but then, his exposure to men of the cloth was very limited. Barrett noticed his assessment and chuckled softly.

"My church is the big red one just past the corner over there." He pointed northward. "If you ever need to talk, or if you need a friend, just call."

"I appreciate the offer." Adam grinned and glanced down at his ankle. "But I'm limited in my social interaction at the moment."

"No problem, I'll come to you." He handed Adam his business card before turning to Laura. "You'll let me know if I'm needed, won't you?"

"Of course."

He started to leave, then turned back. "Oh, I meant to ask you, how's it going with the Keller building? Any luck? I understand the auction is coming up soon."

Laura sighed. "I'm still working on a solution, but at the moment it's not looking good. I'm praying something will turn up because I'm nearly out of ideas."

"Don't give up. I'm sure the Lord is working it out. We just can't see it yet. Well, I'll let you get back to work. I don't want to be the cause of this gazebo not being ready for the festival."

Adam watched the pastor walk away, then looked at his boss. The expression on her face was one of sadness and disappointment. Apparently the little gazebo wasn't the only thing she was concerned with. He started to ask, then thought better of it. "Hey, what's a saw boy?"

She glanced at him and smiled, tugging her hat more firmly onto her head. "You are. You're going to get to cut all the wood on this project."

Adam grinned in anticipation. "We're talking power saws, whirring blades, danger, stuff like that?" Laura grimaced and shook her head, motioning him back to work.

"I was just wondering, how long do you think this job will take?" Adam asked.

"If all goes well and everything arrives on time, two to three weeks. What's the matter, Holbrook? You bored already?"

"No, but I have someplace I need to be at the end of the month. I don't suppose you could put in a good word for me with your uncle? Convince him that the quickest way to get this job done on time would be to hire another professional?"

Laura frowned. "I don't suppose I could. What's so important that you have to be there? Some sort of big celebrity party?"

He should have expected her to react that way. He

doubted she'd be sympathetic to his dilemma anyhow. "Never mind. Forget it."

Adam watched Laura return to the table saw. She was a hardworking, hands-on kind of woman. People were expecting her to restore what had been damaged. She'd find it hard to identify with a guy who never had to question where his next paycheck was coming from. But then, no one had ever expected anything from him. Until now.

Adam rubbed his protesting shoulders and stretched his back to ease the kink in his spine. He'd been working nonstop since the pastor's visit and his body screamed for relief. Almost as much as his stomach craved food. Apparently, Laura stayed small because she never ate. He was beginning to wonder if he'd ever taste food again when he heard a familiar voice call out.

"Hey, y'all. I thought I'd treat you to lunch today." Tom Durrant walked toward them across the courthouse park, a large pizza box in his hand. Laura went to meet him.

"Thanks, Dad. I hadn't even thought about eating. Too much to do."

"Hello, Adam. Is she working you too hard?"

"Nothing I can't handle so far." Adam brushed off his hands and joined them.

"How's it going, Boo?"

"Fine. We should have the damaged section cleared away by tomorrow, then we can get a better idea of what we're looking at." She handed Adam the hot pizza box and turned to give her dad a warm hug. "Thank you, Daddy. You're the best."

Adam watched with interest as the two embraced.

A moment ago Laura Durrant had been all business—determined, focused and self-assured. But she'd turned into a happy little girl when her father showed up. He found himself wondering what other sides there were to his boss.

"Well, I won't keep you. Enjoy your lunch and I'll see you both later at the house."

Laura smiled over at Adam, her eyes bright. "Isn't he just the sweetest? Someday I'm going to find a man just like him to marry."

Adam saw the love and admiration in her expression, feeling sorry for the man who tried to live up to the image Laura had created. Even in the short time he'd known Tom Durrant, he knew he was a man worthy of admiration. But few men on the planet could measure up. Adam held out the pizza. "Where do you want to eat this?"

"Over here." She walked to the truck, lowered the tailgate and hopped up on it, feet dangling. She held out her hands for the box.

Adam joined her, wiping his hands on his jeans. "I thought tailgating was for football games."

"And construction sites. I have some hand sanitizer if you need it."

There was a teasing glint in her eyes. "I'm good, thanks." He took a slice and bit into it with gusto. He couldn't remember when he'd last worked up an appetite like this. He glanced over at Laura. "So, I take it your family is close?"

"We are. My older brother, Matt, lives here in town with his two children. He teaches at the community college. He's getting married next month to his high school sweetheart. His first wife died of cancer."

"That's tough."

"It was, but then Shelby came back to Dover. She'd had some serious health issues and came here to stay with her grandmother while she recuperated. She had no idea Matt lived next door, but once they saw each other again, all the old feelings came back."

"Just like that?"

"No, but they worked things out and now they're getting married. My other brother, Ty, is a cop in Dallas. He's single. He was shot recently and he's still recuperating. We're hoping he'll be able to come home for Thanksgiving."

"What about you? No one special? Like the pastor, maybe?"

"What? No!" Her cheeks turned pink. "He's married. Besides, I don't have time for a relationship. I've got too much work to do. Especially now."

"So what's this Keller building the pastor mentioned? Another restoration project?"

"In a way. See that old building on the corner opposite my dad's store? That's the Keller building. It used to be a pharmacy way back when. When I was a kid, it was a candy store. I've been trying to save it for three years, but nothing has worked out. It's going up for auction in a few weeks and I've run out of options."

"Is there something special about that building, like this gazebo?"

"If you mean is it part of the history of this town, then yes. Is it a landmark? Officially, no. Mr. Keller would never cooperate with getting it designated. He owned that whole block at one time. I've been unable to find funding or grants, anything that will keep it from being sold to some developer who will either tear it down and use it as a parking lot, or put up some kind of modern building that would destroy the charm of Dover."

Adam tried to imagine the corner with a parking lot or a sleek office building. He might not like small towns, but he could fully understand her concern. And he admired her devotion. "What do you plan to do with it?"

"A senior center. A place for them to gather, share their experiences and their life skills with others."

"Interesting."

She shrugged, a small smile on her lips. "I like older people. They are so wise and knowledgeable about life. They have so much to teach us. But most people today are too busy to listen, let alone pay attention." She took another piece of pizza from the box. "As long as we're sharing, it's my turn to ask a question. Why do you do the crazy, risky stunts you do? I don't understand."

"For the thrill. You never feel more alive than in that moment when you plunge down a hillside." He looked into her eyes and the skepticism and disapproval in them pierced his spirit. She'd just told him about wanting to save an old building for senior citizens and he talked about jumping off a cliff. Suddenly his lifestyle felt petty and insignificant.

"Is that the only time you feel alive?"

He didn't know how to answer that, so he fell silent, and took another bite of his pizza, hoping she would move on to another topic.

"Is that all you do? Drift from one adventure to another? You don't have a real job of any kind?"

Adam grew uncomfortable with the direction this conversation was going. He didn't like talking about his personal life and Laura Durrant had a way of making his love of extreme sports seem trivial. "I have a few endorsement deals."

"So, people pay you to wear their clothes or use their gear?"

"That's the general idea behind endorsements."

Laura wiped her hands and took the last swig of her drink. "I thought so. I recognized your type right off."

"Oh, really? What type would that be?"

She counted them off on her fingers. "Never done an honest day's work in your life. Only concerned with your own life. No thought of anyone else. No idea how to love anyone but yourself."

The fierce tightness in his chest made it difficult to breathe. She'd seen through his shield with the precision of a surgeon. When had he become so transparent? He'd have to be more careful. Keep his guard up. He couldn't give her a chance to see any more. "You don't pull your punches, do you?"

"Let me ask you, do you have one close friend? Someone who would stick by you no matter what?"

Adam ran down the list of people he knew, the guys who followed him around. Could he count any of them as a true friend? The truth hit him like a shard of ice in his heart. "No."

"I rest my case." Laura slid off the tailgate and closed the box of pizza. "Time to get back to work. We can't rebuild until we take it all apart."

Sucking in a breath, Adam tried to ignore the sting of his new realization. He had no real friends because he'd never wanted any. Casual friendships were easy to walk away from. Anything more was messy and complicated. But now he wondered what his lack of relationships had really cost him.

Chapter Three

Laura Durrant pulled the truck to a stop in her parents driveway, keeping her eyes straight ahead. Adam reached for the door handle at the same time she started to talk. "We got a lot done today. I couldn't have gotten this far without your help. Thanks, Holbrook, for being so cooperative."

She braved a look in his direction. One corner of his mouth was hooked up into a grin.

"That wasn't cooperation. That was fear. You scare me."

A chuckle escaped her throat. "I doubt anything scares a man who can swim with sharks and run with the bulls."

He leaned forward slightly to look at her. "How did you know about that?"

Warmth infused her cheeks and she shrugged to hide her discomfort. "I looked you up on the internet." Now he would think she was interested in him. No way.

Adam sighed and shook his head. "Ah. A man can't have any secrets anymore." He started to get out of the truck, but when she didn't move he glanced back at her. "Aren't you coming in?"

"No. I need to check on my other jobs." Gripping the steering wheel, she gathered courage. "Holbrook, I want to apologize to you."

"For what?"

"I shouldn't have said those things to you—about you being selfish. That was unkind and judgmental. You worked hard today and you didn't deserve my nasty comments. I'm sorry."

It was clear from his expression her apology had caught him by surprise. He held her gaze a long moment then rubbed his forehead. "It's all right. You weren't wrong. You hit the nail square on the head."

Remorse flooded her conscience. "I'm so sorry."

He shook his head. "It's okay. As a matter of fact, it's nice to hear the truth for a change."

It's not what she'd expected him to say. "What do you mean?"

"Most people I know tell me what they think I want to hear. They don't want to offend the hand that drives the adventure train."

She'd never thought about that side of things. It must have cost him to admit that. What would it be like to know people didn't really care about you, only what you could do for them? "I'm sorry, Adam. I have a bad habit of speaking my mind. It was one of the things my…some people don't like about me." He smiled over at her, causing a small skip in her heartbeat.

"Really? I think it's one of your more interesting qualities." He climbed out of the truck, offering a little salute before shutting the door. She waited while he took the steps to the back porch before backing out of the driveway. Every time she thought she had the guy figured out, he threw her a curve. No one liked her forthright attitude. Why did he?

Adam knew Laura was watching him as he climbed the back steps to her parents' home. She probably wanted to make sure he didn't bolt. Or else she was feeling sorry for him. He hadn't intended to speak the truth but something about Laura made him want to. He was glad to be away from her penetrating assessment.

He reached for the door knob and hesitated.

But he wasn't sure he wanted to be back at the Durrants' either.

Adam grew uneasy at having to walk back into the Durrants' home. Since coming to Dover, nothing he'd experienced was familiar. He didn't like that. He pushed open the back door, stepped into the kitchen and froze.

The air was warm with rich delectable aromas. A woman he'd never seen before stood at the stove. For a second he wondered if he'd returned to the wrong house.

"Oh, hello, Adam. I'm Angie Durrant. Sorry I wasn't here this morning to greet you, but Tom thought it might be more comfortable for you with only him. Sort of a man-to-man thing."

Adam stared at the scene in front of him, trying to process it all. Mrs. Durrant was an older version of her daughter. Slender with short dark blond hair turning gray. Her smile was like her daughter's, as well. It lit up her eyes.

"Oh, don't forget to call the station. Use that phone over there. The number is beside it."

Her thoughtfulness caught him off guard. She'd actually tried to make things easy for him, acting as if she cared about what happened to him. He moved across the kitchen to the desk, noticing the table was set with colorful dishes and bright placemats. This wasn't normal. He placed his call, then turned back to Mrs. Durrant.

"I hope you're hungry."

His stomach answered for him. "Yes, ma'am, I am."

"Good. You have time to clean up if you'd like. Tom will be here in about twenty minutes. Come on down when you're ready."

Fifteen minutes later Adam returned downstairs certain he'd been mistaken about the warm welcome to find only one thing had changed. Tom Durrant was home. They sat down at the table, and after Mr. Durrant had offered the blessing Mrs. Durrant passed the food. He'd never tasted anything so good. Tuna casserole, she'd said. Nothing fancy. But it was definitely on par with some of the haute cuisine he'd tasted in his travels. The conversation revolved around various events in Dover. He answered questions put to him, but offered nothing more. He made his escape as soon as he could without appearing rude, explaining he was tired from the day's work.

In his room he stretched out on the bed, every muscle in his body protesting the abuse he'd given them today. He tried to watch television, but couldn't concentrate. He wanted to sleep, but he was too tired. If only he could get this situation sorted out, find some solid ground to stand on and get through the month. Trouble was, he had no frame of reference. No experience with family and home-cooked meals. How was he supposed to behave here? What did they expect from him? He didn't know how to talk to these people. He'd never talked to his parents. They were never around.

A knock on the door brought him to his feet. He opened it to a smiling Tom Durrant holding a book in his hand. "I forgot to mention that we'll all be going to church in the morning. It's important that you attend." He handed the book to Adam. It was the Holy Bible. "Thought you might need one. This belonged to my younger son, Ty."

"Mr. Durrant, I appreciate what you're doing here—letting me stay with you instead of in the jail—but you don't have to go to any trouble on my account."

"Call me Tom. And I'm not sure what you mean."

"Eating together, fixing big meals, all that. I can take my meals up here. It's not a problem."

Tom frowned. "We're not doing anything differently, Adam. We always have our meals together. Always have. That's what families do. Service is at ten-thirty. Good night."

Adam shut the door, thinking of all the places he'd rather be than with the Durrants in Dover. Bible stuff. He fingered the worn leather cover, an odd tension swirling deep in his gut. It had been a long time since he'd looked at the words inside. A friend in college had led him to the Lord and for the first time in his life he'd felt as if he belonged someplace. He was loved and accepted for who he was. Someone—God—cared what happened to him and had a plan for his life.

Then he'd gone back home. His parents dismissed his newfound faith as a fad that he would hopefully get over. And he had in a way. He'd tried to find a church to attend, but the arguments with his father had escalated. When Adam had declared his intention to live his life in his own way, and refused to go to work at Holbrook Electronics, his father had retaliated by disowning him and placing a restrictive condition on his trust fund that demanded his appearance each year to collect. His father's way of keeping him in line and making him see the error of his ways.

His faith had taken a backseat to his troubles and he'd drifted. But lately he'd sensed the Lord tapping his shoulder, trying to get his attention. Maybe that's why he'd ended up here in Dover.

Laura ended the call to her foreman, Shaw McKinney, and smiled. So far everything was on track with her other jobs. She hoped she would be as blessed with the gazebo project. The last thing she needed was another job. Her schedule was full and teetering on a wobbly budget. She should be helping on the Conrad place or pushing her attorney to settle the Mobile mess. Instead, she'd be spending the next four weeks tracking down two-hundred-year-old timber to replace the damaged wood. The Dover gazebo was one of the few historic buildings in town that was absolutely pristine. The only changes made over the years had been the addition of electricity, which had been upgraded for safety reasons a decade ago. Only the most minor repairs had been necessary. Until Adam Holbrook had come to town.

Pouring a glass of sweet tea, she called for her little dog, Drywall, to follow her out onto the front porch of her house. She settled into the old glider, inhaling the pungent fall air and letting her gaze drift to the small buds that were starting to form on the winter camellia bush at the edge of her porch.

Adam Holbrook hadn't behaved like she'd expected him to. She'd been prepared to prod, threaten and argue about everything she asked him to do. Instead he'd been cooperative and helpful. His reaction to her apology had thrown her a curve, as well. She'd expected him to say something smart, to defend his lifestyle. Instead he coolly acknowledged her comments as truth.

She couldn't figure him out. But it was only the first day. Sooner or later he'd show his true colors and balk at the work. It was all new and exciting to him now, like one of his wild adventures. She doubted he had the staying power or the attention span. He'd grow bored and then she'd be working alone. She felt sure he was incapable of any kind of commitment.

She scratched behind Wally's ears. And yet, there was something about him that hinted at another man beneath his polished exterior. Someone nice. No. She was simply tired and irritated, building castles in the sky, and it was time to go to bed. There was nothing worthwhile about Adam Holbrook.

The knot of tension in Adam's gut tightened as he followed Tom Durrant down the aisle and into a pew midway in the sanctuary the next morning. It had been years since he'd been to church, other than a wedding or a funeral. The Bible in his hand felt heavy and awkward. He could sense the eyes of the congregation on his back, and he was thankful when they finally took their seats.

Adam glanced down at his khaki pants, relieved to see most of the congregation dressed casually. But it was more than his outward appearance that made him edgy. Inwardly he wasn't prepared to sit in God's house. He allowed his gaze to travel around the old church, struck by the eerie familiarity of the place. With its stained-glass windows, carved wood moldings and massive pipe organ, it reminded him of the church he'd attended in college. Strange that he'd find one so similar here in Dover.

Mrs. Durrant stopped at the pew, Adam stood and stepped into the aisle to let her in to sit beside her husband. He took his seat again only to feel a tap on his shoulder a few moments later. He looked up to find a lovely young woman smiling at him. With a shock he realized it was Laura Durrant. She gestured for him to scoot over to allow her to join them. He'd lost his voice. He realized it was the first time he'd seen her without either her baseball cap or hard hat. The hair he'd guessed to be dishwater blond was in reality a rich honey brown with amber highlights. It hung in soft waves, caressing her neck and shoulders like fine silk. The flowing black-and-white skirt flirted around her calves. The white top gently skimmed her curves, something the loose-fitting T-shirts never did. Her violet eyes were wide with thick lashes. The graceful line of her jaw was the perfect frame for soft lips and a tilted nose.

Until now, he'd only seen the stern, no-nonsense contractor. There'd been glimpses of her softer side, but it had been hidden behind her tool belt and power tools. He looked at her again, unable to take his eyes off her.

She frowned at him in disapproval. "What?"

"You look nice."

She blushed and faced forward.

He groaned inwardly. Brilliant. What a dumb thing to tell a woman. When the music started, he sent up a grateful prayer. He needed a distraction. More important, he needed to hear what was said here today. He'd been away from his faith too long. The liturgy unfolded in a welcome and familiar way, creating a deep ache in his chest. Pastor Jim's words hit their mark in his spirit as he spoke of the rich young man who asked how to gain eternal life, but when told he had to give up his possessions and follow the Lord, had turned away.

The story could have been his own. He'd found his faith, but once away from the campus and out in the real world, he'd drifted away. Now, he felt an over-powering need to reconnect and restore the faith he'd been ignoring.

Laura stood when the pastor called for prayer, uncomfortably aware of Adam Holbrook beside her. Dressed in a white long-sleeved shirt and khaki pants he didn't look much different from the other men in the church. And yet, he did. The white shirt highlighted his deep tan, reminding her that he spent a lot of time outdoors. There was a crisp, clean look to him today that was ridiculously attractive and appealing. Each time she inhaled she drew in the tangy scent of his aftershave. She was grateful when the music started. She was in church to worship. Not admire a man. Her voice faltered, however, when she heard Adam join in the praise song. He didn't sing loudly, but he knew the words and he had a nice singing voice. A rich baritone that flowed over her senses like warm honey.

Her mind churned with questions. She hadn't expected him to know anything about church, but he focused intently on the service, never taking his eyes from the pastor. She breathed a sigh of relief when the service ended. She needed to put some distance between herself and her new saw boy.

As the congregation started to file out, her father reached over and touched her arm.

"Will you take Adam to the house? Your mom and I need to meet with the worship committee chairman for a few minutes. We won't be long."

Laura nodded, hiding her reluctance behind a smile. She glanced up at Adam to find him smiling down at her. She searched for something to say. "You have a nice singing voice."

He chuckled softly. "You didn't think I'd know how to behave in a church, did you?"

"No, that's not true."

Adam leaned down and spoke softly into her ear "It's not nice to lie in church, Boo."

Her cheeks flamed. She opened her mouth to deny it, but remembered his comment about people telling him what he wanted to hear. "No, I didn't."

Adam chuckled deep in his throat. "I'm a believer, Laura, just not a very faithful one." They stepped into the aisle, Adam placed his hand lightly on her back and they made their way to the door. "I had a friend in college who brought me to the Lord. I was pretty active for several years."

"What happened?"

"I graduated."

She started to ask more questions, but they'd reached the door and the waiting pastor. She shook Jim's hand and moved through the doorway, waiting for Adam. He stood in front of the pastor a long moment. Jim nodded a couple of times, then smiled. Adam joined her, a thoughtful look on his face. He looked down at her, his gaze probing and slightly amused. Her heart quickened. Suddenly, being this close to Adam Holbrook was not a good idea. She turned and hurried to the truck.

* * *

Adam eased back out of the Durrants' crowded kitchen and found a spot in the adjoining family room where he'd be out of the way. The aroma of roast beef and steaming vegetables sent his taste buds into overdrive. All his other senses were being bombarded, as well. From the moment he'd stepped into the Durrant home after church, the house had been buzzing with activity. Laura had stopped by the gazebo to check on things before going on to her parents' house. He'd found it distracting, trying to reconcile the woman he'd worked with yesterday with the lovely woman who'd sat beside him in church. Being in the close confines of the truck cab had only highlighted the difference. A difference that made him curious about this new side of Laura Durrant.

Angie Durrant caught his eyes and smiled. "Adam, could you come and give us a hand?" He swallowed the knot of unease in his throat but obeyed. Laura handed him a potato peeler and a spud when he joined her at the large center island. He stared down at the items in his hands. He'd peeled a potato. Once. He heard Laura chuckle and glanced over at her. Her violet eyes were sparkling with amusement.

"Like this." She demonstrated the technique quickly and handed the items back to him. "Then cut them into pieces and drop them into the pot on the stove."

He did as he was told, but when he put his pieces of potato in the pot, they didn't look the same. He turned to Laura to inquire, but she was hurrying from the room.

"Matt and Shelby are here, Mom."

He searched his memory. Matt. The oldest brother who was getting married to his former sweetheart.

Angie Durrant wiped her hands on a towel and hurried to the hallway. Adam sought out his little corner in the family room. No need to intrude on family time.

Before he could take a few steps, the women were back, forcing him to stop and get caught up in the moment.

Mrs. Durrant touched his arm gently and smiled at the tall man who came into the kitchen. "Adam, this is our oldest son, Matt. Matt, our houseguest, Adam Holbrook."

Houseguest? He appreciated her not spelling out his situation. Matt extended his hand and shook Adam's hand. "Nice to meet you."

He resembled a younger version of Tom.

"And this is his soon-to-be wife, Shelby Russell."

The elegant brunette smiled, but didn't shake his hand because her hands were full of a pie and a basket.

"Hello. Could I get you to take one of these, please?"

Adam relieved her of the pie, setting it down on the only clear spot in the kitchen.

He turned around to find a little boy staring up at him. He had green eyes, sandy hair and a nose full of freckles. "Hello."

"My name is Kenny. What's your name?"

"Adam."

"Like in the Bible." Kenny frowned and wrinkled his nose. "There aren't any Kennys in the Bible."

"I don't think I've ever heard of any," Adam admitted.

"Are you the man who broke the gazebo?"

Adam's felt a rush of embarrassment warm his face. "Kenny."

Adam glanced over at the boy's father, who looked

as embarrassed as he felt. No sense in trying to hide his guilt. "Yes, I am. I wasn't paying attention and I wrecked it with my car."

Kenny looked up at him with sympathetic eyes. "Sometimes I don't pay attention. I get in trouble a lot. But it's okay because my daddy loves me anyway. That's what daddies do."

A large knot formed in the center of Adam's chest. It was hard to find his voice. Not all daddies. "That's good."

A young girl joined the boy. "Hi, I'm Cassidy. Aunt Laura is helping you fix the gazebo, right?"

"She is."

"Good, because we like to hang out there a lot and now we can't."

Shelby Russell came and steered the children to the other room with instructions to set the table.

Adam glanced around the kitchen. Everyone was going about their business, not paying any attention to him at all. Suddenly, he wanted out. Away from all the warm and cozy nonsense. He tried to battle his impulse to flee. He wanted to go to his room to sort things out, but to do so would be rude. He took a step backward, seeking distance. Everyone seemed happy, even joyful. It couldn't be real. Did every happy family act this way?

Angie Durrant caught his attention, motioning him to the kitchen. She handed him the bowl of rice and smiled. "Go put that on the table then tell the boys we're ready to eat."

He nodded, wondering for the tenth time how he ended up here. He'd never felt so out of place, so awkward, in his whole life.

Were they trying to rehabilitate him? Were they trying to make him feel the burden of his damaging their landmark? Or was it money? Did they think he would compensate them later for their kindness? The thought immediately filled him with shame. These people weren't like the ones he normally associated with. The Durrants were people he had little exposure to.

Adam placed the bowl, then moved slowly into the family room. The guys were focused on the Saints football game. "Food's ready."

Matt turned and smiled. "'Bout time. I'm starving." He punched his dad playfully in the arm. "Chow."

Tom stood and tapped his grandson, Kenny, on the head. "Come on, kiddo."

Adam followed them into the dining room, a strange tightness in the center of his chest as he watched the family come together. Laura smiled and motioned him to the seat beside her.

He asked himself again if what he was seeing was real. Probably not. They were all on their best behavior for his sake. Trying to put on a show. The way his parents did whenever they came home. Once a year his mother would parade out her best china and invite the crowd. They'd all smile, put on a display of family happiness, then the next morning, they'd all go their separate ways.

Something told him this family wouldn't change with each day. How did they do that?

Tom Durrant bowed his head and stretched out his hands. Before Adam could register what was happening, Laura took his hand in hers, completing the circle around the family table. The room was suddenly hot. His hands began to sweat and he wished he could let go of Laura's hand, but to do so would be rude. He inhaled a slow breath and tried to focus on the grace being said.

"…for family. For your sacrifice and redemption and for never-ending love. Bless our guest. We ask that you make his time here a benchmark for his life. Amen."

Adam wanted to ask Mr. Durrant what he meant by benchmark, but he didn't feel comfortable doing so. He'd only been here a day and a half and he'd never been so unbalanced in his entire life. He could face any danger, risk his life on the flimsiest of whims, but spending an afternoon with a real family left him tense and edgy.

The moment the prayer was over, Adam released Laura's hand, surprised to find his fingers missing the contact. Her hand was small and deceptively delicate, but he was well aware of the strength, as well. He'd seen her in action. She could handle power tools with the best of them. This was the first time he'd seen her in a more domestic setting. She looked at home here, too.

"So, Adam," Matt said, once dinner was under way, "Laura tells me you're some kind of daredevil?"

Adam spared a quick glance at Laura. "I wouldn't say daredevil. I participate in various extreme sports. I like adventure. I want to experience life to the fullest."

"How does your family feel about your dangerous pursuits?"

Mrs. Durrant's question blindsided him. He'd never considered their feelings before. Adam looked at the expectant stares. *They don't care.* Swallowing his hurt, he forced a smile. "It's not a problem."

"I've read about you," Matt said, gesturing with his fork. "There was an article in an issue of *Sports Lookout* a few months back. You were in Nepal, rafting."

Adam nodded, remembering the roar of the white water and the ache in his arms from fighting the force of the river. Then there had been the rush when he'd thought they were going to crash into the rocks. "That was a wild ride."

Matt chuckled. "I'll say. I'm afraid I don't have that kind of courage." He reached over and took Shelby's hand. "I've got too much to lose."

The smile on Adam's face froze. What did he have to lose? Nothing. If he'd died in that river, not a soul would have shed a tear. His death would have made headlines. His funeral would have been well-attended, but not a person on earth would have cared.

"It's a unique lifestyle," he muttered, trying to wipe the picture of Matt and Shelby's loving glance from his mind.

Conversation drifted to other topics, for which Adam was grateful. Normally he loved entertaining folks with his adventures, but his exploits seemed out of place here. Everything he said felt contrived against the simple, honest lives of this family. He was more determined than ever to get out of here. He didn't belong here. He didn't belong anywhere.

"Old family tradition," Tom announced when the meal ended. "The women cook, the men clean up."

Adam followed the men's lead, stacking plates and silverware and taking it to the kitchen. Even little Kenny carried his own plate from the dining room.

It wasn't like he'd never cleaned up after himself. His adventures often took place in locales with few amenities. It was the sense of inclusion that made him uncomfortable. The Durrants all behaved in a way that assumed he would participate. No formal invitations. No awkward suggestions. Merely the understanding that since he'd shared a meal he would, of course, share the work.

The gesture made him uneasy. He could chitchat with the rich and famous, but he had no idea how to talk to a pair of regular guys.

Tom pulled down the dishwasher door and slid out the rack. Matt began scraping the dishes. Kenny and Adam finished clearing off the table.

"Didn't I read that you jump out of helicopters?" Matt asked.

"That's right."

"Cool," Kenny gushed.

Adam shared the finer points of heli-skiing with the guys. To his surprise he found a new kind of delight in telling the stories and seeing their reactions.

Once the dishes were done, Kenny urged them outside for a football game. Kenny wanted to be on Adam's team which made him nervous. He didn't want anything to happen to the boy. It didn't take long for him to get the gist of football Durrant-style. All the roughhousing was done with great enthusiasm and flourish, but with care and restraint. The result was fun for all and Kenny felt like he'd played with the big boys.

Adam had played plenty of pickup games with his buddies, but never had he enjoyed a game as much as this one. Tom came up and placed a hand on his shoulder.

"Good game."

"Thanks. I think Kenny had fun."

Tom chuckled. "Yeah. We play a bit differently when he's in the game. You should see us when my younger son is here. He's over-the-top competitive."

Adam did a quick search of his memory. The brother who was a cop. "I hear he's doing better."

Tom turned serious. "He is, but there's still a long way to go."

"Sorry to hear that."

"The Lord will work it out. We have to leave it to Him."

"What if He doesn't work it out the way you want?" He regretted the question the moment it was out of his mouth. These people had been generous and hospitable to him today and he was questioning their beliefs. "I'm sorry. I shouldn't have said that."

"It's all right. It's a valid question and you're right. The Lord may not work it out the way we hope, but He'll work it out. Maybe better. Maybe different. Either way, we have to trust that He had the best plan for my son. God sees the whole of Ty's life. We see only a small part."

"So you're saying, no matter what the future holds for your son, you're okay with it?"

Tom shook his head. "Not okay, but at peace. The Lord may be teaching Ty life lessons for some future purpose that I know nothing about."

He'd wanted to ask more, but the family was congregating in the kitchen again, talking and laughing. The kids were squealing for dessert. Angie was cutting the pie and giggling with Shelby and Laura. Suddenly the commotion was overwhelming. He had to get away and think. Find someplace quiet to regroup. Going to his room was out of the question. He'd have to walk past them all and explain why he was leaving. He caught sight of the back door and he remembered the patio. Slowly he moved away until he was just inside the small mudroom leading to the back porch.

Quickly he ducked out and hurried down the steps,

making a beeline for the far end of the patio and the bench that circled the large oak tree. He sat down, taking a few deep breaths, placing one foot on the bench seat and closing his eyes. Never in his wildest dreams would he have thought that being around a family would be more stressful than jumping out of a helicopter or skiing down a mountain.

He took a few deep breaths, letting his heart rate slow and the tension ebb away. The cool evening air helped settle his muddled thoughts.

"Are you all right?"

He jerked his eyes open to find Laura standing in front of him. Even in the fading light he could read the concern in her violet eyes. "Yeah. Just tired, I guess. This is all new to me."

"You mean the carpentry work? You'll get the hang of it. You did great yesterday." She sat down beside him and he felt his heart speed up again.

"No, not that. It's all the family stuff. It's different."

Laura looked at him curiously. "We're just an ordinary family. Nothing different about us."

Adam shook his head. "No, not like any family I ever knew."

"What was your family like?"

"Nonexistent." He laughed to make light of it, but he knew she wouldn't let it pass.

A frown creased her forehead. "Are you an orphan?"

He shook his head. "Just an only child." She waited and he knew he had no choice but to satisfy her curiosity. "My parents don't really live together. I don't think they ever did. My mother has her life, my father has his. Once or twice a year we'd meet at the old family mansion and throw a big dinner party. Everyone would make nice, brag about their latest exploits, and then in the morning, go their separate ways."

"Well, who did you live with? Your dad?"

The laugh escaped before he could stop it. "No. He was working 24/7. And Mom was traveling most of the time." He set his jaw. He didn't like talking about his family or his past. "I went to boarding school or sleepaway camp." He lowered his leg and turned to look at her. Her lovely eyes were filled with compassion. For him.

"I'm sorry. I guess I forget that not all families are like ours. It's all I've ever known. For what it's worth, sometimes I need to get away from them, too. That's why I have my own home."

"Adam, Laura. Dessert is on the table," Angie yelled from the house.

He was grateful for the interruption, but he wanted to talk about her, to learn more. They started back inside.

"Don't let them get to you. Take them in small doses. Mom with smother you with food and kindness if you let her. She'll be all up in your business. And Dad watches everyone like a hawk. You're under his roof, so you're one of his for the time being."

"And I'm working closely with his baby girl."

"Yeah. You figured that out, huh?"

Her smile turned a light on behind her violet eyes. She was so lovely. So easy to talk to. He'd have to be careful. She had a way of seeing through him. He had to remember his only goal was getting home in time. He *had* to find a way to make that happen.

Chapter Four

Laura curled up on the sofa, patting the cushion to signal for Wally to join her. The little buff-colored dog buried his nose in her hand, begging for love. She couldn't help but smile. He always put her in a good mood. "You're such a sweet boy, aren't you?" She stroked the soft fur, her eyes on the television, but her mind on Adam Holbrook.

She was more confused than ever about him. He'd been full of contradictions today at her parents' house, one minute helping as if he belonged and then other times tense and withdrawn. Several times she noticed him pull back, watching the activity from a safe distance. At first she'd thought he didn't like her family. But then she'd glimpsed something in his dark eyes, a shadow of longing, a flash of puzzlement. His comment about his family and childhood haunted her. Nonexistent. Was he serious? If so, her heart ached for him.

She couldn't fathom such a life. She was so close to her parents and brothers. They got together as much as possible, helped each other, comforted each other. Of course, it wasn't all roses. Mom could be a meddler at times and Dad tended to be overprotective where his kids were concerned. She and her brothers got along most of the time, but there were petty issues that caused differences of opinion now and again. Matt was way too uptight and serious. Tyler was hotheaded and easily angered. She'd been the fixer, the one who wanted to save things and make things better. But they were family. First and foremost.

Her cell phone rang and she scooped it off the end table, smiling at the name on the screen. "How did you know that I needed to talk to someone?"

Shelby, her soon-to-be sister in law, chuckled. "Just a feeling. Actually I wanted to see if you wanted to go with me to look at wedding flowers next week. I need to decide what I'll carry down the aisle."

"Of course. Just let me know when." There was a slight pause.

"I also wanted to ask you about your new hired hand. I know he nearly destroyed the gazebo, but he's seriously good-looking. You might have trouble concentrating on your work."

"Aren't you about to marry my brother? You shouldn't be noticing other guys."

"I'm engaged, but not dead. He might be handsome, but he can't hold a candle to my Matt. No one could. Seriously, though, what do you think of him?"

"He's an entitled rich guy who only thinks about himself. Been there. Done that."

"You mean Ted, your ex? Is he really that bad?"

Laura sighed. "Okay, he's not that bad. He's actually been easier to deal with than I'd expected."

"Well, Kenny and Cassidy thought he was way cool. Kenny hasn't stopped talking about him."

She had a point. The kids had followed him around like little groupies and he'd treated them with kindness at every turn. She'd seen his joy in participating in the family football game, and her brother and dad had both treated him like one of their own.

"Matt and I liked him right off. And from what I saw, your parents like him, too."

That left her as the only one with doubts. Maybe Shelby could help her sort things out. "He told me our family wasn't like anything he'd ever known."

"What did he mean?"

"I think we made him uncomfortable. He said he was raised in boarding schools and rarely saw his parents because they were too busy with their own lives."

"How sad. Though, I have to tell you, the first time Matt brought me to your house on a Sunday I was totally intimidated. I can sympathize with Adam."

"I guess we do take a little getting used to," Laura said.

"You know, I think he's attracted to you, Laura. I saw him watching you a couple times today."

"No way. I'm his boss. Besides, I'm not his type. I'm sure his taste in women runs toward sophisticated and wealthy. Maybe even a supermodel or two."

"Laura, don't put yourself down. You're beautiful and sweet, and somewhere out there is the perfect man to appreciate you. Maybe he's right there in your father's house. Oh, sorry, I've got to go. Cassidy is picking on Kenny again. Time to play referee. I'll talk to you tomorrow."

Laura hung up the phone, shaking her head at the nonsense Shelby had spouted. Adam was *not* attracted to her. Sure, he'd actually opened up to her and told her a bit about his life. But that didn't mean he was interested in her.

She stood and headed to bed. Adam Holbrook was not attracted to her. Besides, the only men she wanted in her life were skilled workmen, not some self-centered adventurer. Right?

The room was closing in on him. He'd been here with the Durrants for three nights now and he still felt awkward and on edge. It was a nice room. Spacious and comfortable, but it wasn't his room. It belonged to a stranger. Everything in this house was strange to him. He was used to hotel rooms, or tents and huts on the way to his latest adventure. He even felt at home in the most luxurious of homes, but he didn't feel any more comfortable in this happy family homestead.

His gaze landed on the trophies lovingly and proudly displayed on the dresser. Matt was a grown man with a family, but his parents still cherished his accomplishments. Adam had no idea where his trophies were. Tossed in a closet? Thrown in the trash? He couldn't remember either parent looking at one.

He stretched out on his side, surfing through TV channels as a distraction. He was dog-tired and sore all over. The hot shower had helped, but now he couldn't relax. He needed to sleep if he was going to keep up with Laura tomorrow. For such a little thing she had more energy than five men. Though she treated him like he was incapable of doing anything without her detailed instructions. She'd been telling him for two days she'd teach him to use the saw, but so far he hadn't touched anything more than a crowbar and a hammer.

He was anxious to show her he had some aptitude. All he needed was a chance to prove it to her.

He looked at Laura differently since Sunday. She'd been relaxed and happy, moving with a grace and femininity that mesmerized him. She'd laughed with her mom as they prepared dinner. Teased her brother mercilessly and played with her niece and nephew. During the football game, the women had cheered the men on and he'd found himself looking in her direction to see if she was watching him.

Over the past couple of days on the job, she'd stopped and spoken a kind word or shared a hug with nearly everyone who had passed by the gazebo. There appeared to be no end to her caring nature. Love came naturally to her.

Which only made him more aware that he didn't belong in Dover or with the Durrants. He needed to get home. Maybe it was time to eat crow and call his ex-girlfriend/lawyer, Gail. The thought didn't sit well. But he didn't belong here, and if he didn't get home in time, he wouldn't belong anywhere.

Laura parked the Handy Works van in her dad's driveway and honked the horn. She hoped Adam was ready because they had a lot to do today. The old bricks had arrived on time and her brickmason, Tony Donato, would be hard at work for the next couple of days bringing the foundation back to its former glory. The damaged section of the gazebo had been dismantled, stabilized and all the pieces catalogued.

Adam hopped into the passenger seat, glancing around the large vehicle. "What's this? Aren't we working today?"

She shook her head. "Tony is starting the foundation repairs. That will take a couple days." She looked over at him and raised her eyebrows. "Today you start the community-service phase of your sentence."

He frowned. "Let me guess, serving up soup in a kitchen or picking up trash along the highway?"

"Neither. Something much more fun and educational."

"Now I'm scared. Like what?"

"Have you ever done any plumbing?" She glanced over at him, choking back a giggle at the look on his face.

"You're kidding."

"Nope. And we have a long list of good deeds to do today."

"Good deeds?"

"That's right. We'll be doing a few Handy Works projects for the next few days."

"Handy what?"

"Handy Works is a ministry my brother and I started. We do repairs, chores and anything else people need who can't afford to hire the work done or are unable to do it themselves."

"And you do this because?"

"We're called upon to help those less fortunate. Didn't your mother ever teach you it's better to give than to receive?"

"No." He looked away. "Like I said, she wasn't around to teach me anything."

Her cheeks burned with remorse. She realized that Adam always used the past tense when speaking of his mother. "I'm sorry. When you talked about her the other day, I didn't realize she was dead."

"She's not. She's in Thailand lounging on the beach. No, that was last month. This month I think it's Australia."

Laura stared over at him. He was completely cool and indifferent when he spoke about his mother. She'd found his comments about his parents so hard to believe that she'd convinced herself he had been exaggerating. Now she had to consider he might be telling the truth. "Surely she was home when you were little."

"Nope."

"Then who raised you?"

Adam exhaled a bitter laugh. "Nannies. Seven, if I remember correctly. What's our first stop?"

How sad. His parents absent from his life, never experiencing the closeness and love of a family all added up to a picture of neglect that made her heart ache. She was a soft touch for anything or anyone who'd been neglected. She'd have to watch herself. Adam wasn't an old building or house she could restore. He was only a man passing through her life. She wasn't God. She couldn't restore people. In a few weeks he'd be gone.

Later that morning Laura backed the van out of the narrow potholed driveway of the Randall home, bracing herself for what she knew was coming. The repairs on the bathroom had been hampered by a drunken and belligerent Mr. Randall. It had gotten so bad that at one point Adam had been ready to plant a fist in the man's face. It was her reminder that punching Mr. Randall would only lengthen his stay in Dover that had stopped him.

She knew he had a mind full of opinions to spew. It was easier to let him get it out than try to restrain him. She'd barely cleared the drive when he cut loose.

"Why are you helping a man like that? He's a lazy bum. He doesn't deserve any charity. All you're doing is making it easy on him."

"I didn't do it for him. I did it for his wife and children. They deserve running water. They deserve to live in a house that has a working toilet. Or would you have me let them suffer because he's a jerk?"

Adam stared out the window a long moment before answering. "It doesn't seem right."

Laura understood his outrage. It was hard for her, too. "Yes, Will Randall is a mean drunk. No, he doesn't provide properly for his family, but that's not the issue. Our ministry is to help, not judge or rehabilitate or condemn."

Adam sighed and propped his foot on the dash. "Who's next on our charity list?"

"Edith Johnson's house." She pointed ahead a few houses. "She needs a wheelchair ramp built from her front porch to the driveway."

"Doesn't she have family who could do that?"

Laura nodded. "But one son lives in Vicksburg and the other is in New Orleans. They've been trying to coordinate their schedules, but they have teenaged kids. It's hard. She finally called and asked us for help."

"So you step in like a fairy godmother."

"No, as a friend wanting to help. Sometimes people are too proud to ask. As Christians, we're called upon to help those less fortunate."

"Handy Works, you mean?"

Laura glanced over at him, gauging his expression. He seemed sincere enough. "Yes, I wanted to do something to help."

She parked the van and got out, walking up to the

house. Adam followed at a distance. She knocked. The door opened slowly, a face peered out through the narrow opening. "Miss Edith? I'm Laura Durrant from Handy Works. We're here to build your ramp."

"Oh, bless you." The little woman cooed happily. "I'm so glad you're here." She opened the door wider, making way for her walker. "I'm so ready to get out of this house and I can't until I have a ramp."

Laura entered the house, stopping just inside the door. "Are you doing better? I thought you were confined to the wheelchair?"

"Oh, no, not all the time. I'm supposed to use this contraption as much as possible while I'm home." She jiggled her walker slightly. "But if I leave the house I need the chair. The senior shuttle won't pick me up unless I have a ramp. All my friends are going to all sorts of exciting places and I'm stuck here."

Laura patted her arm. "Not for long you aren't. We'll have that ramp done this afternoon. You'll be ready to run the roads with all the other girls."

Edith giggled. She glanced at Adam. "Who's your handsome friend?"

She'd almost forgotten about her shadow. "This is Adam Holbrook. He's going to help me build your ramp."

Edith nodded, studying him closely. "You're the one. I heard what you did." She shook her head, making a clicking sound with her tongue. "It's good that you have to fix what you've broken, young man."

"Yes, ma'am."

Laura appreciated Adam's respectful tone.

Edith smiled then and reached over and patted

Adam's arm. "You're a good boy. I can see it in your eyes. You just need some attention."

Adam didn't respond and Laura seized the moment. "Well, we'd better get started. You go on about your business and we'll check in with you on our progress."

Back at the van, Laura opened the double doors and stepped inside. "You grab the worktable, I'll get the circular saw." Adam followed directions without comment. Within minutes they had the work area set up. Portable workbench. Table and miter saw. Lumber.

She instructed Adam on how to measure for the ramp and how to figure the correct grade to prevent the wheelchair from rolling too quickly. "First rule. Measure twice. Cut once."

"Sounds redundant."

She couldn't tell if he was being sarcastic or not. "You miscut a piece of lumber, you waste money, material and time."

"Got it. So when do I get to cut?"

She had to let him do it eventually, but she hated turning her tools over to someone else, especially a novice like him. But she needed his help and for that he had to learn to handle the equipment. Resigned, she picked up a couple pieces of scrap she'd brought along for just such a purpose. She placed a section of two-by-four against the fence of the miter saw and stepped back. "Okay, hold it firmly in place, grip the handle, pull the trigger first, then lower the blade."

Adam looked uncomfortable, but he did as he was told. Laura watched carefully.

"There." He held up the severed board. "How's that?"

"Okay. Do it a few more times until you get the feel of it."

Adam smiled after cutting his fourth piece. "I like this."

Laura frowned. "It's the easiest one to use. Next up, circular saw."

"I'm ready." He rubbed his hands together eagerly. "Bring it on."

Twenty minutes later Adam made his first real cut. He surprised her by doing it quickly and correctly. With his help, the base for the ramp was completed in short order. He'd measured wrong only once. Laura tugged on her cap and wiped her forehead. "All we need now is to cut the plywood to fit and Miss Edith will be set free from her home. Go get a piece of three-quarter-inch plywood out of the van and bring it over here while I set up the saw."

Laura adjusted the blade angle, then glanced at the van. Adam was walking toward her, the four-by-eight sheet of plywood balanced against his shoulder. The muscles in his arms strained against the weight. His long, sure stride accentuated the powerful legs.

She told herself to look away, but she couldn't. He was the very image of masculine power. Of course he was in good condition. He'd have to be to pull off some of the fool stunts he did. Laura gritted her teeth and forced herself to look away. She couldn't deny Adam Holbrook was an attractive man. Too attractive. Which had nothing to do with anything.

Adam held the edge of the plywood as she guided it through the table saw, taking its weight as the blade did its work. He set it aside and followed Laura to the ramp base. Pulling a handful of screws from her apron, she handed them to Adam. She'd have preferred to use her nail gun, but the nail gun required a compressor and the van they were in today didn't have one.

Adam set the last screw, then stood and stretched. "Is that it? We done?"

Laura slipped her hammer into her holster. "We just need to get Miss Edith's approval." Laura knocked on the door, eager to see the smile on her face. She wasn't disappointed. The older woman touched the rail tenderly and shook her head in disbelief.

"You did it so quickly. Thank you so much. Oh, I have something for you both." She disappeared inside briefly, then emerged with two small bags. "Please accept these in appreciation for all your hard work. I know you won't take any money, but what you've done for me is such a blessing that I can't let you go without saying thank you in some way."

Laura took the two small bags with pleasure. The chocolate-chip cookies were still warm from the oven. She wrapped her arms around the slight woman in a warm hug. "It's our pleasure, Miss Edith. And thank you for the cookies."

Once in the van she handed Adam one of the bags. "If you want a thrill, then you need to bite into one of those. No one makes cookies like Miss Edith."

He examined the bag of cookies. "Do the people being helped contribute anything to this arrangement?"

"Like what?"

"Money. To help with the costs."

Laura shook her head and started the engine. "Handy Works is a volunteer organization. We rely on donations to keep operating so we don't have to ask for funds from those needing help."

"That doesn't sound like a good business plan."

"We're not in it to make money. We're in it to help others."

"But you get nothing in return."

"Oh, I get a great deal in return. You just can't put a price on it. We're a charity, not a business."

"I understand that, but who pays for the supplies, the gas for the van? What if no one volunteers one day? What then?"

"It's worked so far."

"I'm just saying there might be a better way to do things and still keep it voluntary, but provide you a little financial security, as well."

"You sound like my dad."

"From what little I've seen he appears to be a good businessman."

"He is." Her father had always told her if she got the same advice from two different sources, she should pay attention. But why did one of those sources have to be Adam Holbrook?

Adam leaned back in the large chair in his room and bit into one of the homemade cookies Edith Johnson had given him, slowly savoring the taste. He loved chocolate-chip cookies. He'd tried every brand on the market. At one time he'd even had the nation's undisputed best cookie, Jamison's Premier, shipped to him wherever he was in the world.

But he'd never tasted anything like the ones made by the little old lady he'd met today. They weren't the biggest or the most visually appealing. They were small and misshapen. But the melt-in-your-mouth, deep chocolate taste was amazing. All that was lacking to make it perfect was a big glass of milk.

In the time he'd been living with the Durrants he'd never left his room once he'd retired for the night. He didn't want to intrude into their private time and he didn't want to call attention to the fact that he was technically a prisoner in their home. Angie had repeatedly told him to make himself at home, but he'd never taken her up on the offer. Until tonight.

Moving to the door, he cracked it open, listening for sounds of activity. Quiet as a church. He eased out and went down to the kitchen. Taking a glass from the cupboard, he poured some milk and sat down at the table. He'd eaten two cookies when Tom entered the room. He glanced up, prepared to apologize, but Tom held up his hand and took a seat at the table. Adam offered him a cookie.

"Oh, Edith Johnson's, right?" He pulled one from the sack and took a big bite. "Wonderful. Was this your reward for doing community service? Homemade cookies?"

Adam grinned. "Unusual but effective."

"I'm guessing this is a new kind of charity work for you."

"You could say that. I usually write a check or make a pledge. Sometimes I attend a gala charity party."

"Those are all good ways to help others, but using your own two hands, actually doing the work that's needed, that's a different thing entirely."

Adam understood the concept. He'd learned long ago that watching someone do extreme sports bore little resemblance to experiencing it firsthand. "I'm starting to understand. Can I ask you about Handy Works? How can it keep going if you rely only on donations and volunteers? Even the best of charities require some form of financial base to operate. Laura's ministry wakes up each morning not knowing whether they'll be able to do business that day or not. I just think there might be a better way to structure Handy Works and keep it volunteer-based."

Tom studied him a moment. "I agree, but I have to let Laura do it her way for now. In case you haven't noticed, my Boo is a very loving and giving young woman. She's also very passionate about anything she takes on."

"Oh, I've noticed." She'd worked on the ramp with her usual energy and dedication, wielding power tools and a hammer with gusto. Then she treated the elderly Miss Edith with the gentle love and care of a nurse.

When she smiled, it was as if a light came on inside her. She glowed with happiness. The woman's joy over her new ramp was reflected in Laura's violet eyes. Laura had said her payment had nothing to do with money. He was beginning to understand. The satisfaction she received from the project was larger than the ramp she'd built for the older woman.

"I understand you have a conflict with the length of your sentence."

Adam shifted uncomfortably. He was learning quickly that nothing was secret in a small town. "I do. My father and I haven't been on good terms for a long time. When I refused to go to work in the family business, he cut me off. Left me a trust fund, but I have to show up in person each year to get my paycheck or I lose it all. This sentence won't be over until two days after the deadline."

"So you come from a family-owned-business background like Laura does."

The comment caught him off guard. He'd never

thought about it. "Yes, I suppose so." Holbrook Electronics had been started by his grandfather. He was the
third generation, but he wanted no part of the business.
Was that why his father had put the conditions on his
inheritance? Had he been hoping that his son would
eventually see the value of his legacy and join the team?

"Parents have expectations for their children. Some
men work to build a business with the goal of creating
it to pass on to their son. If the son doesn't want it, then
it can feel like a slap in the face. All their sacrifice and
hard work was for nothing." Tom stood and pushed his
chair under the table. "I'm sorry to hear about your
conflict, Adam. I wish there was something I could
do to help."

"Thanks, Tom, but it's my fault, my situation to deal
with. I'll figure something out." He *had* to. There was
no alternative.

Laura poured water into her coffeemaker, set the
timer and turned off the kitchen light. Tomorrow
couldn't happen unless the coffee was ready and waiting when she got up. Today had been a good day. The
brickwork was coming along and both Handy Works
projects had gone well. Adam had been more help than
she'd anticipated. He'd never complained. Never refused
any task she'd assigned. Though he was totally puzzled
by the Handy Works ministry.

She'd been blessed to be able to make a living doing
work she loved and to be surrounded by people who
cared about her. Her ministry allowed her to help others and give back.

She let Wally out the back door, waiting on the stoop
while he attended to his business.

But was that enough? She'd been content with her life until Matt and Shelby had gotten engaged. Lately she'd been wishing for someone to come home to. Someone other than a dog.

An image of Adam Holbrook came to mind—his make-your-knees weak smile, the broad shoulders that had come in handy today. Good grief, what was she thinking? "Wally, come on."

The moment the dog returned, she closed the door. The wedding, that's what was causing all these crazy thoughts in her head. Seeing her brother and Shelby so in love and planning their wedding was making her all dreamy.

The phone rang and she ran to get it. "Hello?"

"Hey, Boo. You have time to talk to your old dad?"

"Of course. What is it?"

"I learned something today that I think you should know about. It concerns Adam."

Laura listened as her father explained, her mind trying to absorb what she was hearing. When she finally said goodbye she knew she'd spend several sleepless hours tonight considering his suggestion.

Chapter Five

Laura watched Adam as he came down the back porch steps and walked toward the truck. His usual enthusiasm was missing today. They'd worked together nearly a week now and she'd come to recognize his moods. Normally he jogged down the steps and hurried to join her. Today he was dragging his feet and the relaxed grin he usually wore was missing, as well.

He climbed in and shut the door with barely a mumbled hello. She allowed him some space. She'd been working him pretty hard. He wasn't used to the physical demands of construction work. Maybe it was catching up with him. But her concern mounted when he kept silent for more than a block. "Is everything all right?"

He glanced over at her and nodded. "Yeah. I think the confinement is getting to me, that's all."

"I'd hardly call staying at my parents' home confinement."

"It is when you aren't free to go anyplace but there. Don't get me wrong, I'm grateful to them for taking me in. I'd rather be there than in jail. But I'm used to being on my own, not sharing a house with someone else. I could use a good run. I normally get in five miles a day, but that's out of the question for now."

"I know this must be hard for you, but it can't be helped."

His mouth moved in a small grin. "Time to pay the piper, huh?"

"In a way. If it makes you feel any better, I think you're doing a great job at the gazebo. In fact, if you wanted to put your mind to it, you could be a decent carpenter."

"Thank you. I'll keep that in mind. I might be looking for work soon." He turned back toward the side window, ending the conversation.

Laura thought about what her father had told her last night on the phone. That Adam would lose everything if he wasn't in Atlanta on time. Unfortunately, his deadline was two days before his sentence was over. Her father had offered a suggestion, but she wasn't sure she liked it.

Slowly, Laura drove the truck up over the curb and parked beside the gazebo. The city had removed a portion of the iron fence so she could park closer and keep tools and materials handy. She went immediately to the newly restored foundation and made her inspection. Tony had done his usual outstanding job. The was no sign of the damage.

Now she could start the woodwork. She was looking forward to it. It was what she loved. She hoped Adam wouldn't be a hindrance. If he caught on to everything as quickly as he had during the construction of the ramp yesterday, she might have to revise her opinion of him.

"What do we do today?" He lifted the nail gun from

the truck bed and examined it closely. "This should be a blast to use."

Laura grinned. Typical man. They reverted to ten-year-olds when they had a power tool in their hand. "It doesn't work that way. You can't fire a nail gun like a pistol."

"No? Then how does it work?"

"You have to compress the tip before the trigger will engage."

Together, they worked on rebuilding the floor of the gazebo. A few hours later, Laura decided they needed a break. She brought Adam a cold drink, hoisting herself up onto the edge of the nearly completed deck.

Adam had been very helpful. His strength had made replacing the joists and sistering in supports for the less-damaged ones quick and easy. "I got a call from Edith." She took a sip of her drink. "She loves her ramp."

"Good." He came and sat down beside her. "Have you known her long?"

Laura shook her head. "Not well. I've met her once or twice."

Adam frowned. "I thought you knew everyone in Dover."

"We're not that small a town. Not anymore. I was born and raised here, but I don't know everyone."

"But you like the slower pace, the quiet?"

Laura raised her eyebrows. "That's a misconception about the South. We work just as hard and long as anyplace else. My days fly by faster than I can handle sometimes, and I never feel like I'm going at a slower pace."

"No insult intended. I guess I like the big city because there's always something happening. I like the unexpected."

"I like predictable."

"And that's why I'd go crazy living in a place like Dover."

A small twinge of disappointment settled in Laura's mind. She should have expected him to feel that way, but she'd hoped he was at least coming to appreciate her hometown.

"How did you like Miss Edith's cookies?"

"Fantastic, but they're all gone."

Laura laughed. "They never last long. But don't worry. Miss Edith sells her cookies over at Cynthia's gift shop. We can pick some up next time we're in the area."

"Good, because Miss Edith needs to patent that recipe. She could make a fortune."

"Can't." Laura shook her head. "It's not hers. She uses the same recipe everyone else does, the one on the package."

"Nah, I don't believe it. There has to be some kind of secret ingredient."

Laura chuckled softly. "Oh, there is. It's called love."

"Right."

"Honestly. She loves making the cookies. She loves giving them away. She loves selling them. It's the same way your mother's cooking always tastes better than anyone else's—the love she puts into it for her family."

"I wouldn't know about that." He stood and tossed his empty bottle into the trash.

Too late she remembered his comments about his mother. She bit her lip. She'd have to watch what she said from now on, but it was hard to monitor her words when her life was so full of family.

"I don't suppose there's any way I could get my car fixed before I'm released?" Adam glanced back over his shoulder.

"I wouldn't know."

"Do you have someone around here who knows about vintage cars? That baby's a classic."

"If it was so valuable, why were you driving it in the first place?" She tossed her hammer onto the workbench and picked up her notes.

"I'd just broken up with someone and I was soothing my bruised ego with a new car." Adam set his hands on his hips. "So, what do we tackle next?"

Laura dared a look into his green eyes, darkened now by some emotion. Sadness? Loneliness? He walked back to the workbench, leaving her with questions. It was hard for her to grasp that Adam had never known even the most basic of family experiences. Things she took for granted, like her mother's love and attention, her close relationship with her brothers and being brought up to care for others. Maybe her father's idea had merit after all. It would be a win-win situation for both her and Adam.

As they worked together on securing the final screws into the floorboards, Laura waited for a good time to start a conversation. "When are you supposed to be in Atlanta?"

Adam turned and studied her, his green eyes narrowed. "The twenty-eighth. How did you know about that? Oh, wait. Your dad."

She nodded. "It's important that you get home in time for this meeting?"

"Crucial."

She took a deep breath and crossed her arms over her chest. "I want to propose a deal."

"Meaning what?"

She heard the skepticism in his deep voice and she couldn't blame him. "Maybe there's a way we can both get what we want." She braved a glance at him. His expression was expectant but wary. "Dad talked with my uncle last night and he's agreed to let you out in time for your meeting, but the gazebo has to be done or no deal."

"Is that possible? To finish early, I mean?"

She nodded. "I've got the materials and the subcontractors lined up. If all goes well, we could actually be finished a week ahead of schedule. Plenty of time for you to get home and meet your obligation."

Relief was clearly visible on his face. He dragged a hand along the back of his neck.

"All right, it's a deal." He caught her gaze. "Thanks. This means a lot to me."

His probing gaze made her uneasy and she glanced away.

"Good. Okay." She went back to work aware of his eyes still on her. It hit her then. If they got the gazebo done as quickly as she'd hoped, she'd have one less week to deal with Adam Holbrook. The idea wasn't as welcome as she'd expected.

It had taken them until noon to finish placing the screws to firmly secure the floor. Adam was a big help, even though he still worked slower than her regular guys. She placed her drill bit on the final screw, driving it in with gusto before letting out a triumphant shout. "Done!"

She climbed down and stepped back to admire the work, unable to keep from smiling.

"So what are we celebrating?" Adam came to her side, watching her curiously.

"The floor. We are ahead of schedule. You don't know what a blessing it was to have those oak planks in my shop. Trying to find more would have taken days." She smiled up at him, almost giddy with delight.

He chuckled and smiled. "Okay. If you're happy, I'm happy."

She wanted to dance around the park, but that would be undignified. Her joy evaporated when her cell phone rang and she read the name on the screen. "Oh, no." She answered the call, her mood plunging with every word spoken in her ear. She hung up and sagged against a sawhorse.

"What's wrong?"

"That was the supplier at Ashley Salvage calling to tell me I can't get the cypress I need for the roof. I'll have to find a new source."

"Won't some other wood do?"

"No. I'm required to restore with original materials when possible."

"And when it's not possible?"

"It's always possible. It'll just take longer to find and have it shipped here. I may have to go get it."

"So will this mess up the schedule?"

Laura shrugged. "Not necessarily. I just hope we can keep up this pace. People will be so disappointed if it's not done for the festival."

"Well, then, we'll just have to work harder. What do we tackle next?"

"I have to check on my other jobs. I'm not sure what I'm going to do with you, though."

"Couldn't I tag along?" He straightened, slipping his hands into his pockets. "Wouldn't helping you on other jobs qualify as community service?"

"I suppose so. Okay, I'll get you extra leeway on your ankle monitor, then we'll get something to eat first." Laura crossed her arms and studied him a moment. "Burgers or chicken?"

"What?"

The bemused look on his face made her chuckle. "Well, we have to eat. Might as well do that first. I'm starving." She started gathering up her tools, then climbed into the cab and slammed the door. Adam hurried to join her. She turned to face him, fingers paused on the keys. "What will it be? Burgers or chicken?" The smile Adam gave her sent her heart tripping. It really was a great smile.

"Burgers."

"I know the perfect place. Best burgers in central Mississippi."

"Don't forget to call about my monitor. I don't need to get on the wrong side of your uncle again."

She cranked the engine. "Don't worry about it."

"Easy for you to say."

They rode in silence until they pulled up at a refurbished gas station. The sign read Fill 'er Up Burgers. Adam had to smile at the owner's sense of humor. The old filling station had a lot of charm, from the old gas pumps outside to the vintage car parked as if waiting to be serviced. It was right out of a 1950s postcard.

"Interesting." He smiled as they walked through the

door. The decor inside continued the theme. Hub caps and old license plates adorned the walls. Refurbished motor oil stands and vintage road maps completed the effect. The tables were made of stamped steel. An antique cola chest-type container served as the payment counter.

Adam felt all eyes focus on him the moment they stepped through the door. A hush fell over the diner. He was suddenly more aware of his ankle monitor than he'd been before, even though it was well-hidden beneath his jeans and boots. These people saw him as the bad guy. A destroyer of their beloved landmark.

Laura walked toward a table in a far corner and sat down against the wall, allowing him to sit with his back to the other customers. He relaxed a bit. At least over here he was protected from the accusing stares. "Do they stare at everyone who comes in or just me?"

"It's a small-town thing. They look at anyone who comes in. You just warrant a longer look. Don't let it get to you. They did the same to me when I moved back home. They'll get over it."

He picked up the menu. "I thought you might be trying to put me in my place."

"No. I just thought you might like a good burger. I never meant for this to make you uncomfortable."

Before he could answer, the waitress arrived. "Good afternoon Laura, Mr. Holbrook. What can I get for you today?"

Adam looked from Laura to the waitress. Her tag said Sally. "You know who I am, Sally?"

"Oh, sure." She smiled while popping her chewing gum. "We all know who you are. You gonna have that gazebo done for the festival?"

He glanced around the diner, swallowing the lump in his throat. No way was he going to fail. "Count on it."

Sally pointed her pencil at him, her eyes narrowed ominously. "I'll hold you to that."

They placed their order, and Adam felt himself relax a bit. Apparently the fascination over his arrival had waned. "Clever decor in here."

"Thanks."

"Did you do this?"

"I had a hand in it." She smiled. "Mostly I restored the building."

"Really?"

His simple question opened a floodgate. For the next ten minutes Laura explained with enthusiasm how she saved the old gas station from decay and gave it new life. Adam saw a side to her he'd never suspected. Her eyes sparkled and her face glowed as she described how they'd searched the entire South for the authentic period details. How she'd traveled to Florida to find period tiles to line the walls and how they'd refinished the old metal displays to use as serving stations.

Her passion was overwhelming, born of a deep love of her work. He was envious. He'd never experienced that kind of enthusiasm for anything and now he wondered why.

The food arrived and Adam bit into his burger with gusto, emitting a low groan of appreciation. It had to be the best burger he'd ever eaten. Laura glanced up, her violet eyes sparkling. A flicker of a smile touched her lips and Adam froze. She was lovely.

"I told you they were fantastic."

"Nothing like a good old American hamburger."

"So I guess you've traveled all over the world, chasing your thrills?"

"Pretty much."

She shook her head. "That's not for me. I'm a hometown girl. I like it right here. Surrounded by people I love and a place that's familiar."

"No wanderlust, huh?"

"Nope."

He rested his forearms on the table edge, leaning toward her. "Come on now. You can't tell me you wouldn't like to see other parts of the world, or maybe even do a few of the things I do. Everyone longs for some kind of adventure, even small ones."

Laura toyed with her napkin. "Not really. I'd be too nervous trying to find my way around foreign countries and learn new languages."

"Name one place you'd like to go. I promise not to tell anyone."

"That's easy. Great Britain. I'd love to see all those beautiful old castles."

"I should have figured that. And what about that adventure? What would you do if you had the chance? If you knew there was no way you could get hurt."

Laura stared off in the distance awhile. "Well, I think I'd like to try the zip line. It must be amazing to fly among the trees, sailing in the air. But I don't think I'm brave enough."

Adam laughed out loud. "Are you kidding me? You manage a successful construction business, climb up on roofs and handle power tools that would make most women faint, and you say you're not brave? That sounds plenty brave to me."

"Maybe, but sometimes I think I took the easy way out."

"How so?"

"I told you I studied architecture in college. I married a man whose father owned a prestigious firm in Houston. We were going to be this great team, designing wonderful buildings. I thought I wanted to live in the big city, away from Dover. But it didn't work out that way."

"What happened?"

"My husband didn't want to actually work in the family business, he only wanted to enjoy the financial benefits. He also decided I was a bit too unsophisticated for his taste. I tried to fit into city life, but I was pretty much a fish out of water. When the marriage ended, I ran home. The rest you know. I haven't been very adventuresome since."

He reached over and touched her hand lightly, staring into her lovely violet eyes. "You're wrong. You are adventurous every time you start a new project."

She held his gaze a moment, then slipped her hand away. "Those are adventures I understand. The surprises are things I'm pretty sure I can deal with."

"Maybe you'd feel differently if you could travel with someone who knew how to speak the language and navigate the unknowns. Someone who could hold your hand each time you encountered a new surprise."

"That might make things easier. I might be braver if I wasn't alone."

"Since when do you have time to sit down and eat?"

Adam looked up at the man who had stopped at their table. He smiled down at Laura, nudging his glasses up on his nose.

"Greg, it's so good to see you."

Adam glanced from the bright smile on Laura's face to the matching one on the stranger's. The man was medium build, medium height, medium all around as far as he could see. Nothing worth causing such a warm reaction.

Laura scooted over, indicating for the man to join them. Adam frowned. He wasn't sure he wanted to share his lunchtime with anyone.

"Sorry, I can't." The man waved off the invitation. "I'm running late as it is. I just wanted to say hello."

Laura stood and hugged him. Adam listened as they discussed Handy Works and something called Martha's House. When she finally thought to introduce him, he was unable to even fake a warm greeting, despite the man's sincere handshake and the obvious way he chose to not comment on Adam's status as the town villain. He didn't like Greg.

He watched the man leave, noting with irritation the warm smile that lingered on Laura's face. He stabbed a French fry. "So who's the boyfriend?"

"He's not a boyfriend. Only a good friend, but he's a remarkable man. He started Martha's House to help battered women. What he's been able to accomplish in the past few years is amazing. I really admire him."

Adam grunted. "What's so admirable about him? He seems pretty ordinary to me."

"He has a heart for others. He gives of himself one hundred and fifty percent. You don't find many people with that kind of dedication and commitment. I doubt you'd understand."

He killed another fry. "I understand more than you think." Is that the kind of guy she liked? Nerdy. Altruistic. He stared at her a moment. Did she think he wasn't giving his all to his sentence? For some reason he didn't want to examine, he wanted her to praise him the way she had this Greg guy. It was time to show Little Miss Contractor what he could really do.

Adam looked out the window as Laura slowed the truck and pulled between two brick pillars holding an intricate iron gate. The Conrad place was an impressive old plantation on the outskirts of Dover. Most of the architecture he'd seen in the small town consisted of Victorian styles and early-twentieth-century homes. Laura had assured him there were newer parts of Dover, but with his electronic leash he'd probably never see those parts of town.

Laura pulled around to the rear of the house and parked. He'd seen a lot of magnificent homes in his life, but this one was impressive with its massive columns on three sides and the intricate iron railing on the balcony.

He followed Laura across the wide brick sidewalk to a smaller house nestled under the trees. Construction noise filled the air. He glanced back at the plantation. "You're not working in the mansion?"

"No. The owners have brought in special craftsmen from overseas to handle most of the restoration. This is Catalpa Grove Plantation. It was the largest in the area at one time. Our job is this smaller building. Originally it was the dowager's house, where the grandmother would live. But the owners want this to be their actual dwelling. They plan on opening the mansion as a bed and breakfast."

From the moment Adam stepped into the work zone, he felt the tension spike. Three men halted their work as if by command and turned to stare at him. All of them looked to be six feet tall and close to two hundred pounds. It felt a little like facing a hungry shark without a cage.

"Don't stop on my account, guys." Laura smiled and motioned them all back to work. "We're behind schedule, remember?"

The men returned to their work. Adam smiled. One word from Laura and grown men toed the line. One man stepped away from his work and came toward them. He stood an inch or so taller than Adam, with a stern expression and sharp features. He was built like a navy SEAL he'd once gone diving with. Not someone you wanted to rub the wrong way. From the daggers shooting from the man's dark eyes, Adam figured it was already too late. The man stopped in front of them, placing himself slightly in front of Laura.

"Shaw, this is Adam Holbrook. Adam, my foreman, Shaw McKinney. Those two over there are Jay Barton and Chris Storm."

The men barely glanced his way. So much for Southern hospitality. Adam offered his hand to McKinney, somewhat surprised when he shook it. Their gazes locked as they sized each other up. Adam had the feeling he'd come out on the short end of the stare-down. The foreman clearly saw himself as guardian to his employer.

He kept out of the way as Laura and Shaw moved about the room. Laura asked questions, for which it appeared Shaw had a ready answer. Adam watched her with fascination. As he'd suspected, she knew how to handle the workmen, somewhere between firm and respectful, but still displaying a no-nonsense attitude that reminded them who was in charge.

Laura moved off with the foreman into another room, leaving Adam to explore on his own. He was careful to keep a safe distance from the burly men working around the room. His carpenter skills were insufficient to tell if the men were doing a good job or not. But he doubted if they'd do less than their best with Laura as their boss. The work he saw here was more detailed and refined than what he was doing on the gazebo. He doubted he'd ever have that kind of ability.

Laura's laughter preceded her into the room and Adam spun around to see her and the foreman return. Something about the guy set this teeth on edge. He was too tall. Too rugged. And he didn't like the way the man held Laura's full attention.

Normally he didn't care a hoot what women thought of him. So why did he suddenly care what Laura thought? This small town was doing strange things to his head. Being on a short leash didn't help either.

Adam turned and went outside to wait near the truck. He'd seen enough for today. One thing had impressed him and he wanted to ask her about it. He brought it up as soon as they pulled out onto the street "So how do you do it?"

"Do what?"

"Keep those big guys in line? They have a lot of re-spect for you."

"I'm good at what I do. That's the main thing."

"Is that all?"

"I mastered the mommy stare."

She grinned over at him, the pretty smile causing him to lose his train of thought. "What?"

"You know that look your mom always gave you when you'd messed up? That stern, 'You're standing on my last nerve' glare that said you'd better shape up or face the consequences? My mom could get us kids to behave with one quick look."

"I don't know what you're talking about."

"Didn't your mom ever—" She paled and looked away. "I, uh, just glare at them and they tremble in their boots."

Adam remained quiet for the rest of the afternoon, content to ride with Laura as she did a few errands. He got a quick peek into her workshop when she went to check on the progress of some custom cabinets, followed by a stop at the drive-through at the bank. Finally a stop at McCarver's Millwork to see about the gazebo spindles.

He had no idea how complicated woodworking could be and he wanted to learn more. He wanted to learn more about Laura, too. He'd never met anyone like her. And he was growing more and more fascinated with her each day that passed.

"How are the repairs going?" Angie Durrant finished wrapping colorful paper around a small container, placing it with the others on the kitchen table.

Laura had invited her mother over to work on decorations for Shelby's shower. She'd also wanted to talk to her alone. With Adam in her parents' home she never had the opportunity.

"Good, but not as fast as I would like. Tony rebuilt the foundation, and I already had the oak planks, so we were able to repair the floor joists and the decking. If things go as planned we might actually finish early.

But I still need cypress shingles for the roof, and I need some large pieces of oak so new posts can be turned. I'm not having any luck finding that so far."

"How's Adam working out?"

"He's a big help and he's a quick study. I think if he put his mind to it, he could be an excellent carpenter. Though I don't see that happening. Woodworking doesn't have the same thrill as surfing a fifty-foot wave in Waimea."

"You don't like him?"

"I do." She shrugged. "I guess. He's been polite, helpful."

"But he reminds you of Ted and that makes you nervous."

Her defenses went up. "No. Okay, maybe, a little. Every time I think he might be a decent guy, he'll do or say something that reminds me he's from a different way of life." Laura frowned and pushed the colored paper away. "I mean, when I ended a bad relationship, I bought a business. When he does, he goes out and buys an expensive toy car. Who does that?"

"You know, your dad and I never liked Ted. We didn't think he was right for you or that he treated you with respect. But we didn't know him as well as you did, so we trusted your judgment."

"And I was wrong. Believe me, I won't make that mistake again."

"Aren't you? You're putting Adam into a cubbyhole before you really know him."

"Mom, he's a big-city guy, a man who travels the world. He told me in no uncertain terms he could never live in a place like Dover."

"My point is, don't let one mistake push you too far

in the opposite direction. Your father and I like Adam. I think he's a good man deep down. But I think he's been hurt somewhere along the way."

Laura told her mother what Adam had shared with her about his parents.

"Oh, that breaks my heart. Maybe his time with us, working with his hands, getting to know you, will turn him in a new direction. We'll pray for him."

She shrugged off her mother's concern. Her mom saw only the good in people. Laura had learned to be a little less gullible. While her mother was praying for Adam, she needed to pray for herself. Because she was attracted to Adam Holbrook and she couldn't be. He was all wrong for her. In a myriad of ways. But letting that attraction for a handsome man go any further was not only stupid, but also dangerous. She had to be careful and guard her heart. Because she didn't want to get it broken a second time.

Chapter Six

Daylight had faded into deep twilight, leaving a hazy glow over the neighborhood. Adam stood on the back porch of the Durrants' home watching Laura and Shelby back out of the driveway. They were going to Laura's to work on wedding details. Matt and the kids had left earlier. This Sunday had been different from the first one he'd experienced with the Durrants. There had still been a hearty meal, but only he and Mr. and Mrs. Durrant had shared it. Laura, Matt, Shelby and the kids had dropped by later in the afternoon and they'd all visited over a rich apple dessert Mrs. Durrant had made. It had been a more quiet and relaxed time today.

A small part of him was disappointed there'd been no big family gathering, no football game. Which made no sense at all because he'd felt so awkward and out of place last week. Still, he'd found himself looking forward to the commotion. There had been a moment today, as he'd watched the Durrants sitting on the back porch talking, when he'd been overcome by an odd sensation. As if someone had pulled back a curtain and revealed his deepest dreams, his secret longing. Needs so hidden and long denied even he hadn't realized what they were. But in that instant, he'd known what he'd wanted—a home. A woman to love him. Children.

For the first time in his life he'd found something he couldn't buy. Something he wanted more than anything he'd ever known. He wanted what Laura had. He wanted a home and a family.

He made a fist and thumped it against the porch post. He had to get control of his emotions. He had to stop thinking about Laura. Because the hard truth was he had nothing whatsoever to offer her. He rubbed his forehead, battling the strange churning in his gut. He needed to get out of this small town. He wasn't cut out for family dinners and ball games with little kids.

"Adam, I brought you some tea."

He turned and took the glass from Angie. "Thanks." She sat down in one of the cushioned patio chairs, motioning for him to join her.

"This is always a bittersweet time on Sunday for me. I love having my family around, but I'm always tired at the end of the visits. Getting older, I guess. But then once they're gone, I feel the quiet of the house, and the silence is sometimes as loud as the clamor when they're here."

Adam studied her a moment. She'd read his mind. Put into words what he'd been feeling.

"How are you and my daughter getting along?"

"You want the honest truth?"

Angie laughed. "Please. I'm her mother. I'm well aware of all her flaws."

"Things are better between us now. I had my doubts in the beginning. She was pretty irritated with me."

"Furious might be more accurate."

"Has she always wanted to be a carpenter? I know it's not all that unusual these days, but she seems too—"

"Feminine? I know. She wanted to be a ballerina when she was little. But she also followed her daddy around from the time she could walk. She wanted to dress like him, talk like him. She mimicked everything he did."

He remembered the look of adoration he'd seen on her face when she looked at her father. "He's a shining knight in her eyes. I feel sorry for any man who tries to take his place."

"I worry about that myself. But I think when she finds the right one, she'll have a new knight to love."

Adam stared into his glass. "I can't quite figure her out. She's a contradiction. One minute she's this tough, determined builder, wrangling the burly men of her crew, the next she's pouring out love and kindness to an elderly stranger."

"My Laura has a heart for others. She wants to take care of them, fix things for them. When she gives her love to someone, she gives it completely. And when her heart is broken, it takes a long time for it to heal."

Adam looked at Angie. Was she warning him to stay away from her daughter?

"Did she tell you she'd been married?"

He nodded. "She mentioned that it didn't work out well."

"It shook her self-confidence, damaged her image of herself. Starting her business did wonders, but I worry that she uses her business to keep from finding love again. She needs someone to remind her how beautiful and special she is."

Was she suggesting he should be the one or warning him to steer clear for someone else? Like Greg or the foreman?

"Well, I'm going to pull my husband out of his office and force him to watch a DVD with me tonight." She stood and placed a hand on his shoulder as she passed. "Good night, Adam."

The conversation with Angie Durrant replayed in his mind as he tried to sleep. She'd said Laura loved completely. He didn't doubt that. He'd seen her with dozens of people over the past few days—she loved everyone and everyone was drawn to her. The only people drawn to him were those who wanted something—to bask in his fame or siphon off his money. They hung around as long the fun lasted then went off in search of more stimulating companions. And he hadn't cared.

Until now. He was drawn to Laura Durrant, but at the same time she intimidated him. He didn't understand his conflicting emotions. She wasn't his type on so many levels. But something about Laura made him want to be a better person. She made him believe he could be different, that he could change.

But people didn't change like that. Did they?

Adam secured the last plank on the scaffold, then leaned his arms on the metal railing and looked down at Laura, who was assembling the smaller scaffold inside the gazebo. Time was moving quickly. He was well into his sentence now. And while he still went to bed each night physically tired, his muscles no longer protested. In fact, he felt more fit than he had in years.

From his vantage point near the top of the gazebo, he had a new perspective on the town of Dover. His gaze drifted to the name carved in stone above the door of the bank. He'd have to ask Laura about that name some-time. Everyone pronounced it Dover, as in the White Cliffs of. But the name over the bank read Do Over.

He scanned the area, taking in the now-familiar quaint brick buildings that encircled the town square. His gaze fell on the Keller building. He'd heard Laura on the phone today discussing it with someone. From her expression it hadn't been good news. He didn't un-derstand why she wanted it, but it was important to her, so that was all that mattered. He could understand why she liked it here. There were more than enough old buildings and houses to keep her happy. But was that all she wanted? To save the next run-down store or abandoned church? She was meant to have a family, yet he'd never heard her speak of that kind of future.

"Adam? Would you run over to Dad's store and get a package of blades for the saw?"

He climbed down from the scaffold and joined her at the workbench. "Alone?"

She turned and nodded. "It'll be fine."

"If you say so." He'd come to accept that things were done differently here in Dover. "What kind of blades? Is there a particular one?"

Laura removed the broken blade from the recipro-cating saw and handed it to him. "Show him this. He'll know what I need."

Adam shrugged and started across the park toward Durrant's Hardware on the far corner. He knew finding the right materials for the restoration wasn't going as well as expected. He'd seen a deep sadness in her violet eyes today that had touched off that unfamiliar surge of protectiveness in him. She loved the old gazebo and took a deep pride in repairing it. If it wasn't completed in time for the big town party, she'd take it personally. That knowledge made him want to work harder to ensure her success.

At the corner, Adam waited for the light to change, suddenly overcome with an almost-intoxicating sense of freedom. If it weren't for the weight of the ankle monitor, he could almost forget he was on a legal leash. He had to admit, though, he was starting to get the hang of this carpentry thing. He'd never tell Laura, but he was looking forward to seeing the little gazebo completed.

He stepped into the entrance of the hardware store, glancing down at the tiny black-and-white mosaic tile on the ground. Pushing open the door, he stepped back in time. Durrant's Hardware was a museum.

Wooden floors, warped and creaking, moved gently under his feet. Bins with glass tops lined the center aisle. To one side were long counters in front of wall shelves filled with boxes. On the other a wide staircase with a giant arrow on the wall directed customers looking for paint and tile to go to the second floor. He continued on toward the back where a more modern sign announced the checkout counter. Laura had told him her father would either be there or in his office at the very back of the building.

As he strolled through the antique surroundings he began to realize that the old stuff was merely window dressing. The merchandise itself was up-to-date. Tom Durrant had managed to keep the historic feel of the hardware store yet incorporate all the modern elements needed to run a successful business. He wondered if Laura had been responsible for the decor the way she had made the old gas station into a hamburger place.

"Adam, what can I do for you?" Tom Durrant extended his hand across the counter. "Let me guess, Laura sent you for supplies."

Adam nodded, handing over the broken blade. "New blades for the reciprocating saw."

Tom strolled off a few feet to fill the order.

"Nice place. I feel like I'm in a time capsule."

"Guess who we have to thank for that?" Tom smiled.

Looking around, Adam asked, "So was this a family business, before you, I mean?"

"My dad started the store after World War Two. He died when I graduated from college, so I took it over."

Adam thought back to Tom's comments about fathers leaving their businesses to their children. "I guess your kids will take over after you retire?"

"No, none of them want it. Matt's pretty well set since he sold his business in Atlanta and started teaching. Laura is content with her career and my son Ty is a policeman to the core."

A heavy sadness settled on Adam's shoulders. He hated to think of this unique place being sold away from the family.

"There you go. Tell my daughter I put it on her tab and that it's getting bigger by the day."

"I'll do that." He took the bag and decided to brave a question.

"Are you disappointed that your kids don't want your business?"

Tom exhaled audibly. "Well, I'd be lying if I said no. I didn't have any huge career aspirations when my dad died. I was content with running the store. I'd like to see one of the kids keep the store going, but as their father, I want them to do what they feel called to do. The

Lord's given them each a talent and they should use it. I don't want to derail that out of petty pride."

Adam sorted through Tom's comments as he started back to the job site. He'd mentioned petty pride. Was that at work in his father? Wounded pride and shattered expectations because his son hadn't followed in his footsteps, or had there been something else in his mind? Had he merely been, like Tom Durrant, disappointed that his only child didn't want the business his family had labored to build? Hadn't he wanted what was best for his son?

"Oh, good, you're back. I need your help with the trim."

Adam handed her the bag, reaching for his tool belt. "So why don't you want the store?"

She turned and frowned. "What?"

"I asked—"

"I heard you. Why are you asking?"

"Your dad and I were talking about it."

"I don't want to be a merchant. I don't want to own a store. I have my own business to run and I love what I do."

"What will happen to the store when he retires?"

"I don't know. He'll sell it, I guess." She glanced across the green. "I thought about it. But…" She turned back to the workbench. "He understands."

"Probably. But does he like it?"

Adam reached for the right angle and a carpenter's pencil. His conversation with Tom had given him a new viewpoint on things. Like God-given talents for one. What were his? Did he have any? It never occurred to him to look. Laura had hers. Her siblings had found theirs. What did he want more than anything? What did he want to do? He turned and looked at Tom Durrant's store. Could he be happy here, owning a little store?

It was nearly noon when Adam felt the scaffold shift. He'd been working on removing the damaged shingles. He looked over to see Laura climbing up, one hand holding a large paper bag. He recognized it as the lunch her mother had packed for them this morning.

"Lunch break. Mom's meatloaf."

He helped her get settled, dangling her feet over the edge of the scaffold, then joined her. "I figured out pretty quickly that if I compliment your mother's cooking in the evening, then I get to have it again for lunch the next day. Not a bad deal."

"You found her weak spot."

"Can you tell me what that is about?" He pointed toward the east side of the square. "The Do Over on the bank?"

"Oh, that's the real name of our town. Its original name was Junction City. It was a crossroad between the railroad and the wagon trails to the river. It burned down and the residents decided that because they had a chance to do it over they'd make it worthwhile. So they named it Do Over. Over time the name was shortened to D'Over, then eventually just Dover. The bank's the only building that still has the original name on it."

Adam took another bite of meatloaf. Do Over. He had a funny feeling that God was trying to steer his life, give him a do-over. But how could he be sure?

The foot traffic on Peace Street and the now familiar groaning school buses told Adam the day was winding down. He turned off the table saw and inspected the end of the board, smiling when he felt the smooth even cut. He was definitely getting the hang of this saw-boy thing. He started toward the gazebo to brag a little, but Laura's shout sliced into him. He dropped the wood and hoisted himself up into the gazebo.

Laura was staring at her hand. The sight of blood flowing down her fingers turned his stomach. "Laura, what happened?" He moved toward her, taking her wrist in his hand to assess the damage.

"I went to pick up this piece of lumber and caught my arm on something." She brushed tears from her cheek. "I can't believe I was so careless."

He held her hand, inspecting the cut. "It doesn't look too deep, but that's going to hurt for a while. You have a first-aid kit in the truck?" She nodded and started to move. He wrapped his arm around her shoulders and led her to one of the benches on the undamaged side of the gazebo. "Sit still. I'll get it." Quickly he ran to the truck and returned with the small medical kit.

Adam sat beside her, taking her arm in his hands and carefully cleaning the wound. He applied a disinfecting ointment, then added a bandage to keep it clean. He looked at her, suddenly finding it hard to breathe. Her violet eyes were bright with unshed tears, her mouth was in an adorable pout. He cleared his throat. "I think you'll live."

She smiled at him, her voice husky. "Thanks."

Adam held her forearm, unwilling to let go. Her skin was warm and soft and he could feel her pulse under his fingertips. He'd worked side by side with her for over two weeks yet he'd never been this close to her—their faces only inches apart. She was smaller than he'd realized. "You might want to have that looked at."

She shook her head, her gaze locked with his. "I

get cuts and scrapes all the time. Just part of the job. I should have paid better attention."

"Please be more careful. I don't like seeing you hurt." He couldn't resist the impulse to touch her tear-streaked cheek. He saw her catch her breath as his fingertips met her skin. "Promise?"

She nodded and pulled her arm from his grasp, quickly moving to the edge of the gazebo. She jumped down to the ground and picked up her tablet.

He took a deep breath, attempting to slow his racing heart. She may be all right, but he wasn't sure he'd be. Laura was getting under his skin.

He found it hard to concentrate now and was eager for the day to end. Adam cut a section of trim and turned off the saw. He started toward the scaffold to hand the piece up to Laura.

"Hey, up there."

Adam turned at the sound of a female voice and saw Shelby Russell and Kenny Durrant coming toward the gazebo. Laura leaned over the top of the scaffold and shouted back. "Hi. I'll be right down."

Shelby stopped at the orange fencing. Kenny waved, bouncing up and down on his feet in excitement. "Hi, Mr. Adam."

"Hey, Kenny." He joined the visitors at the safety fence, keeping one eye on Laura as she climbed down the scaffold.

Shelby waved up at him. "Hello, Adam. How's it going?"

"Slow. I've got a lot to learn."

"Lucky for me he's a fast learner." Laura leaned over the fencing and gave Kenny a hug.

"Can I help do something, Aunt Laura? I learn fast, too."

"I know you do, but there are a lot dangerous things around here, and I don't want you to get hurt. That's why we have the fence up, so people won't get hurt."

Kenny pouted, looking longingly toward the tools and materials just outside his reach. Adam inclined his head toward the truck. "Didn't you say you needed a small door for the crawl space under the foundation? I could use some help picking out the best pieces." Laura looked at him with a puzzled frown before she caught on.

"Oh. Right. There are some scraps in the truck. Maybe you can piece it together from those. Kenny, why don't you help him?"

"Cool."

Adam motioned the boy to join him at the makeshift gate on the other side. He heard Laura mention something to Shelby about invitations as he walked away. Kenny skipped happily along beside him as they went to the truck.

"Can I use the 'ciprocating saw?"

Adam stopped in his tracks. "How do you know about those?"

Kenny shrugged. "My grandpa sells them at the store."

"Right, I forgot. No, we won't be using any tools right now. But I will need some strong muscles to help me carry this wood."

"I got muscles. See?" He held up his arms to show off his six-year-old biceps.

"Impressive." Kenny kept up a steady chatter as Adam selected the pieces of wood. He'd hand them to the boy, who would run them over to the fence and pile them up one by one. Adam had more than enough to build the small door, but he was getting a kick out of watching the boy have so much fun. "I think we have all we need. Let's see what we can do about making a door." They started back toward the fence.

"See that pond over there?" Kenny pointed to the opposite corner of the park. "Sometimes my daddy brings us here to feed the fish. You scared the fish when you broke the gazebo."

"What do you mean?"

"Cassidy and me were feeding the fish and then there was a big boom and your car crashed and stuff flew up in the air and scared the fish. Scared me, too."

Cold shock seized his heart. "You were here the day of the accident?"

The boy nodded. "It made a big noise."

"Kenny, let's go." Shelby called to him and waved.

"Bye, Mr. Adam. Can I come help you again?"

He struggled to find his voice. "Sure. You're a good helper."

Kenny dashed off to join Shelby. Adam fought to pull air into his lungs. His heart pounded violently in his chest. Shame and horror filled his head. Quickly, he strode to the other side of the truck, seeking privacy. He laid his palms on the fender, bowing his head, willing his stomach to stop churning.

For the first time since the crash, he truly saw the magnitude of his carelessness. Suddenly there was a flesh-and-blood consequence to his actions. How could he have been so stupid? Unfortunately he knew the answer. Because up until now he'd never had to face his mistakes. He'd paid his way out and gone on to the next thrill.

"Oh, God. Forgive me."

Laura was right. He was self-absorbed. A man with no thought for anyone but himself. He wanted to walk away, leave Dover and never come back, but he was stuck here. Maybe if he talked to Pastor Jim. Maybe he could help him sort it all out....

Laura waved goodbye to Kenny and Shelby. She'd lost track of time. Nora Gibson, the woman who was doing Shelby and Matt's wedding cake, had stopped by to talk and Laura had lost sight of the fact that she should be working. She turned back to the gazebo but didn't see Adam anywhere.

She started back toward the work area, catching sight of him on the other side of the truck. She rounded the tailgate and stopped. Adam had his forearms on the front fender, his head bowed. Slowing, she moved toward him trying to decide whether to speak or wait for him to acknowledge her presence.

She stopped at his side, resisting the urge to touch him. "Adam, are you all right?" He looked over at her and the torment in his eyes pierced her heart. "What's wrong?"

He straightened. "Why didn't you tell me your niece and nephew were in the park the day I crashed my car?"

Laura took a moment to gather her thoughts and calm her racing heart. "At first I didn't think you'd care. Then later, you and Kenny had hit it off and well, I didn't want to upset you."

Adam shook his head and turned away, running a hand through his hair.

"I'm sorry, Adam. I guess I should have said something, but…"

He whirled around and came toward her. "I'm the one who's sorry, Laura."

He took her shoulders in his hands, staring at her with dark, troubled eyes. "I would never hurt anyone, especially your family. And I would never hurt you."

Laura felt tears form behind her eyes. She could feel his hands trembling against her shoulders. She'd never imagined he'd be this upset. It broke her heart to see him this way. "I know that, Adam. I do."

Suddenly he pulled her close, holding her tightly against his chest, his chin resting on the top of her head. "Forgive me?"

She nodded, unable to speak. She allowed her arms to move around his waist. The sense of comfort and belonging she felt wrapped in his arms had cracked open a wall deep inside she'd long ignored. She breathed him in, letting herself imagine sharing his embrace every day.

He pulled back, his gaze drifting downward to her lips, and lingering. She held her breath. Waiting. Part of her brain warned her to stop him, but another part longed to know his kiss. He bent his head, his breath caressing her mouth. Then he pulled back, his hands gently squeezing her shoulders.

"I've already made one mistake today. I don't want to make another." He stepped back and walked away.

It took her several seconds to gather her composure and join him at the table saw. "We could knock off early today if you'd like." She fully expected him to refuse. He never wanted to stop working.

"Yeah, maybe we should call it a day. I won't be

much use to you." He started to unplug the tools and dismantle the portable table saw.

Laura worked beside him in silence. Something had happened between them today and she needed time to sort it all out. Seeing Adam so vulnerable and emotional had demolished all her perceptions about him. And the man she'd glimpsed just now was more unsettling than the cocky daredevil had ever been....

Chapter Seven

Laura pulled on her work jeans, inhaling the sweet autumn breeze that drifted in through the window. The day had dawned clear, cool and with a gentle breeze from the Gulf to make it a perfect day. She'd not slept well, her mind filled with dreams of brides and flowers and a gazebo draped for a celebration. Obviously the result of spending so much time helping Shelby with her wedding plans.

She ruffled Wally's fur, then moved to the dresser for an LC Construction T-shirt. She stopped, the shirt halfway out. On impulse she shoved it back in and opened the next drawer. The pale green scooped-neck T-shirt fit her better, yet was still loose enough not to be suggestive.

For some reason she felt like dressing more feminine than usual. She moved into the bathroom and ran a brush through her hair. Maybe she'd leave it down today instead of knotting it up on the top of her head so it would fit under her cap. Her hand was on her makeup bag when she realized what she was doing. Idiot. There was no point in letting herself be attracted to Adam Holbrook. He was a temporary presence in her life. A man who craved excitement and adventure, who by his own admission could never survive in a small town like Dover.

But from the moment she'd seen Adam standing in her brother's old room, his easy charm and his self-assured attitude had left her feeling edgy and uncomfortable. She hadn't been able to ignore the way he looked at her and the way that look made her feel.

Adam saw her as a woman first and a contractor second. Her crew never saw her as a woman and she liked it that way. She was their boss, doing a man's job in a man's world and she dressed the part. Jeans, boots, tees, flannel in winter. Hard hat and baseball cap. She couldn't do her job effectively if she dressed girly all the time.

Except Adam had made her remember how it felt to wear feminine blouses and skirts. She didn't want to feel that way. She didn't want to remember how it felt to be held in a man's arms, to love someone completely. Yesterday had changed all that. Starting with Adam's tender concern over her cut. She glanced down at the bandage he'd applied with such gentleness. She could still remember the feel of his hand holding her arm.

But what had kept her tossing and turning all night had been the moments behind the truck. When he'd pulled her into his arms and held her to his chest. She knew he was expressing his apology, his deep regret for his actions, but that had taken a backseat to the feelings he'd unleashed in her. She'd thought for a moment he was going to kiss her, but then something stopped him. What had he meant when he said he didn't want to make another mistake? Would he have regretted kissing her? Or had he meant that kissing his boss would have been out of line?

Either way, the end result was the same. Adam wouldn't want to get involved with a small-town girl. They were too different, miles apart in what they wanted from life. Unexpected versus predictable. She should be thanking him for keeping things in perspective.

Snatching up a stretchy band, she pulled her hair into a ponytail and changed out of the green top for a comfy large T-shirt. She had only one focus right now and that was getting the gazebo done. She had to stop thinking about what she didn't have. It was a waste of time and energy.

"Nice work." Laura smiled at Adam and gave him a firm pat on his shoulder. The contact sent a quick current along her nerves and she quickly withdrew her hand.

Adam glanced over his shoulder, holding her with his gaze. "Thanks. I'm starting to like the idea of rebuilding the little house. It all started to make sense to me today, you know. I could see how the pieces fit." He straightened and placed the jigsaw on the floor of the gazebo. "It's like folding a parachute. Each section has to be folded in an exact pattern, a precise order. This construction deal is like that."

Laura slipped her hands into the back pockets of her jeans. "Good."

"You ever going to let me tackle something on my own? I think I'm ready."

"Adam, you're an amateur. A talented one, I'll admit, but all you've done so far is to follow my instructions.

Cut here. Nail there. You don't really know the basics of construction. It's more than knowing how to measure and use a circular saw. There's a progression to the work that takes place and you have to understand it from the ground up."

"I know, but I know enough that I could have built that little door for the foundation yesterday if you would have let me. I'm not saying I want to build a deck or house, just something small, one of the Handy Works projects maybe."

Laura shook her head. "I don't think so, but I appreciate your enthusiasm. Let's start packing up. We're at a temporary standstill until I can find the wood for the posts. I want to squeeze in a Handy Works project before lunch and I need to stop by the church at some point and pick up the list of Handy Works volunteers."

"No problem. I'd like to say hello to Pastor Jim."

"Sure." She tried to curtail her curiosity about Adam's relationship with Jim. The pastor had come by the gazebo a couple of times during lunch and the men had sat on the bench beneath the old magnolia tree and talked for the entire hour. Her dad had mentioned Jim coming by the house once or twice to see Adam, but he hadn't elaborated. Were the two men simply friends or were they discussing spiritual issues? She knew it was none of her concern, but that didn't stop her from wondering.

Laura took another bite of her club sandwich, keeping one eye on her saw boy. Adam sat silently across the table, staring out the window of Magnolia Café. She wasn't sure what was eating at him. The Handy Works job had gone extremely well. The family was happy, friendly and very grateful for the help. For some reason Adam had been quiet and somber the entire time, and his mood had carried over into lunch.

"Tomorrow we'll remove the cupola. I have a crane scheduled to lift it off the roof. Jeb Bryant will make the repairs at his shop, then we'll have it put back when the shingles are done."

Adam stared out the window. "How can they do that?"

"Do what?"

"Those people we helped today, the Watkins. They had nothing. A shack. Barely a roof over their head, but they were happy. How can they be happy when they have nothing?"

"How can you be so unhappy when you have everything?"

Adam met her gaze, shaking his head. "I don't have everything."

The hollow tone in his voice pierced her heart. "You have a lot. Two hands. A brain. Abilities you haven't realized."

A sardonic grin moved his lips. "Maybe. But if I don't show up in the hallowed halls of Holbrook Electronics on time, I'll be just like these people you help. Out of work. No money. No roof over my head."

"Don't give up. We can still finish in time for your deadline. We're only a little behind schedule."

He shook his head. "Maybe it's time to be realistic. I need to be prepared for the worst."

Something in the set of his jaw and the odd tone in his voice worried her. "I don't understand why your father would do this. It's so harsh." She couldn't imagine her dad forcing any of his children into anything.

Adam grunted softly and turned to the window. "I think he figured sooner or later I'd come around to his way of thinking and take my place behind the nice little desk he had for me."

"What will you do if you don't get back in time?"

Adam smiled tightly. "You looking for a new saw boy?"

Laura watched Adam position the last stringer for the gazebo steps and secured it in place. As much as she hated to admit it, Adam had cut them perfectly. He was becoming a competent assistant. He had the potential to be a good carpenter, or anything else he wanted.

"Adam, when you're finished, come over here. I want to show you how to use the router." She glanced over at him. He was staring off into the park, an odd expression on his face. "Adam?" When he didn't respond she looked to see what had captured his attention. A woman about her age was approaching the orange fencing, slowly, deliberately, like a model on a runway.

The woman stopped at the fence, her gaze never leaving Adam. "I need to talk to you."

The words were issued as a command but with a definite intimate undertone. Adam put down the drill and stepped over the fence to join her. Laura heard him mutter something before he took her arm and steered her toward the large magnolia tree a few yards away.

Laura tried to focus on her work, but her curiosity was raging. Unable to resist, she gave up and watched the pair. The woman was sleek, polished and reeked of sophistication. Her tailored suit accentuated her feminine figure while still announcing to the world that she was all business. Her three-inch heels made her already-long legs appear endless and her black, expertly styled chin-length hair wouldn't dare move in the breeze. She was the kind of elegant women Ted had favored.

The woman and Adam stood face-to-face. They were too far away for Laura to hear what they were saying, but the body language wasn't hard to decipher. When the woman reached up and touched Adam's chest in an intimate gesture, a surge of jealousy burned in her veins. When Adam wrapped his fingers around the woman's wrist, she had to turn away. She had more important things to do than watch Adam making goo-goo eyes at some high-maintenance city woman.

Picking up the router again, she placed it on the board, unable to remember what she was supposed to do. All she could think of was the vast difference between herself and the woman. Jeans, T-shirts and a faded cap weren't exactly the kind of clothes designed to elicit appreciative glances from men. As an architect she'd worn stylish suits and heels, but construction didn't lend itself to designer shoes and suits.

"Don't worry about it, Gail. I'll handle it."

Adam's voice broke into her thoughts and she turned to find him and the woman approaching the fencing. Adam stepped over it, his eyes locking with hers. He stopped and looked back at the woman.

"Gail, this is Laura Durrant, the contractor."

Laura opened her mouth to speak only to find herself looking at the side of the woman's face.

"You'll call, Adam, when you've had enough of this backward kind of life. You'll be aching for a real adventure and the excitement of the city." With a condescending glance at Laura, the woman walked off, sashaying across the park as if she owned it.

Adam placed his fists on his hips, staring at the ground a moment. "I'm sorry. I shouldn't have called her, but I never expected her to show up here."

"Who is she?

"My attorney, Gail Breckenridge. She's also the ex-girlfriend I told you about."

Laura's heart lurched. "Why is she here?"

"To get me out. But your uncle refused. Besides, I told her I didn't need her help. Not anymore."

Laura wasn't sure what that meant and she was in no mood to find out. Her ego had been trampled enough for one day. "We need to finish these steps. Unless you're expecting more visitors."

Adam shook his head and went back to work.

Adam stole another glance at Laura as she pulled into the driveway of an old carriage house later that day. She'd been aloof, downright chilly, all afternoon. Only answering his questions with short replies and not initiating any conversation. He debated whether to approach her or wait until her mood shifted. He'd decided to wait, but now he feared her mood might never change. He climbed out of the truck, following in her wake as she entered the house. "What are we doing here again?"

Laura didn't look at him. "Making sure the taping and floating are done."

Adam stopped at her side. "Care to translate?"

"Ready to paint."

Once inside Laura made her inspection in silence. When they stepped into a large room at the back of the house, Adam couldn't contain his curiosity. "So what's this going to be?"

"A music studio. The owner is a pianist."

"I wouldn't think this would be a good studio. The acoustics are lousy."

"It will be fine when we get the sound panels installed."

"I thought you had to follow strict guidelines on these old places."

"This property isn't on the National Register. The owner can do as she pleases."

"I can put you in touch with someone at Holbrook Electronics. That's our specialty. Sound systems."

She stopped and face him. "Really? What kind?"

"Everything. If there's a concert someplace, our equipment is there. In music studios large or small, they probably have our systems in place." He could see her weighing his offer.

"It would help keep my budget on track."

"Say the word. Give me the specifics on what you need and I'll make a call."

"I thought you hated your family business."

Adam shook his head. "I said I didn't want to work there. I never said I didn't understand the business."

Laura stared at him a moment, then went back to her inspection. Her cold-shoulder act was growing old. He had to know what was behind it. He stepped in front of her when she headed for the door. "Care to tell me what's wrong? You seem irritated."

"Irritated?" She set her hands on her hips and glared. "Yes, I am. I'm behind on the gazebo, I've been pulled away from other projects and saddled with an assistant who needs to be told step-by-step what to do. Then to top it off, you walk off the job to go talk to Business Barbie, leaving me to do all the work."

Adam rubbed his forehead. He'd had no idea she'd

been so upset by Gail's appearance. "She means nothing to me."

"Oh, I wish I had a dollar for every time I've heard that."

He remembered what she had told him about her exhusband. Maybe Gail's visit had dredged up some old pains. But why was she so upset with him? Unless… "Laura, there's no reason to feel jealous. Compared to you, Gail's a one-dimensional cardboard cutout."

"Which makes me what?"

Adam searched for the perfect word, but the purple sparks shooting from Laura's eyes unsettled him. "Unexpected." He watched her eyes widen, her arms sag to her sides. She held his gaze a moment, then walked off.

"Let's go."

He followed behind, kicking himself three ways from Sunday for his stupidity. There were dozens of words he could have said. Beautiful. Exciting. Fascinating. And he picked *unexpected?* It was going to be a long ride home.

The heavy guilt riding his shoulders was a new sensation. One he didn't like. He'd lied to the Durrants this evening. He'd told them he wasn't feeling well and had gone to his room without eating. Truth was, he was too disturbed by Gail's appearance and Laura's reaction to eat. But now that he was in his room, the walls were starting to close in. He paced a few steps, then noticed the door to the small balcony off his room. He stepped outside, the cool evening breeze filling his lungs. The air here in Dover was clean and fresh, tinged with pine and a sweet fragrance Laura had told him was from the sweet olive shrub.

His gaze drifted from the house next door to the street out front and toward a hazy light of downtown in the distance. He wished he could forget Gail and the way she'd dismissed Laura as unworthy of her acknowledgment. He'd wanted to say something, but it would only have made things worse. Looking back, he wondered what he ever saw in Gail. She was hard, grasping and insensitive. Much like he had been. Seeing her next to Laura, with her warmth and compassion, her vibrant personality, had been like looking at darkness and light. In the past all he'd wanted was fun and the next big thrill. Now he wanted something different, but he wasn't sure how to go about getting it.

Adam was savoring his second cup of coffee in the Durrants' cozy kitchen when he heard the back door open. He saw Laura walking in. She was dressed in a dark blue business suit; the narrow skirt ended at her knees revealing her shapely legs. The jacket skimmed her curves and highlighted the golden color of her hair. He'd seen her dressed up for church, but she'd worn casual things then. This was a different picture. She looked tiny and delicate. He stood and walked over to her. "What's this? I don't think we'll get much work done with you dressed like that. I'll be distracted all day."

She blushed and tucked her long hair behind her ear. "I'm sorry to spring this on you at the last minute, but Mom and I have a meeting with the Mississippi Heritage Trust committee first thing this morning."

"Sounds important." Adam smiled, his gaze traveling upward to her hair again, wondering if it felt as silky as it looked.

"It is. This is my last chance to save the Keller building from auction, so I have to take advantage of it."

"So we'll work this afternoon, then?"

She shook her head, a look of regret clouding her features. "No. In fact we won't be working for a couple of days."

"Days?" A wave of disappointment sent his mood plummeting.

"I'm leaving for Arkansas right after the meeting. I finally tracked down the wood I need for the gazebo posts at a reclamation company in Mountain Home. It's exactly the right age and they have more than I need. I think I'll take it all. I can always use it other places. I'd given up hope on finding oak that old. I couldn't believe it when my contact called last night."

She tugged at her hair again. Was she uncomfortable around him now? Was she thinking of him with Gail? Had his lapse in judgment ruined their relationship? "So what will I be doing in the meantime?"

"Oh, you'll be working with Dad. He has a big Handy Works project he's been needing help with."

"Good morning, Adam. Boo." Tom entered the kitchen, making a beeline for his daughter. He gave her a hug and turned to Adam. "Did she tell you the news? You and I are going to tackle a big project together."

"She did. I'm looking forward to it. No more taking orders from a girl." He smiled and winked, relieved to see Laura respond to his teasing with a small grin.

"Oh, good, you're here." Angie breezed into the kitchen dressed for business, as well. Adam noticed again how much the women resembled one another. He couldn't blame Tom for being protective.

The women gathered up their things and headed for

the door. Adam stepped forward and touched Laura's arm to draw her attention. "Be careful today. I want you back safely. I really don't mind taking orders from a girl." Her violet eyes widened, then she nodded, holding his gaze a moment before following her mother outside.

Adam followed Tom Durrant up the back steps to the house. He'd worked harder today with Tom than he had with his daughter. Now he knew where she got her energy. They'd replaced the roof on a small house from plywood to shingles. Adam had a whole new level of respect for men who did that type of job for a living.

Tom slapped him on the shoulder as they walked into the kitchen. "A few more days like this and you can apply for a contractor's license."

"A few more days like this and I won't be able to move."

Angie Durrant met them with a warm smile and a kiss for her husband. "How did it go today?"

"Thanks to Adam we got the roof done on the Taylor house today."

"Good." She looked around the room. "What's that I smell?"

Tom grinned and placed the small box he'd been carrying on the table. "In grateful appreciation for our hard work, Ida Taylor sent us home with one of her meat pies."

"Oh, wonderful, because I've been gone all day and you were looking at leftovers." Angie took the pie out of the box, the aroma filling the room. "Y'all can take this for lunch tomorrow, too."

"How did the heritage committee meeting go?"

Angie's expression turned regretful. "Not so good.

We tried everything we could to find a way to save the Keller building. Now the auction is in a few days. I just feel so bad for Laura." Angie sighed deeply. "I'll fix a salad with the meat pie and we'll eat as soon as you boys clean up."

Tom turned and left the room, and Adam moved into the family room where his cell phone was plugged in. He'd only made one personal call since he'd arrived here. One he'd come to regret. This call was different. The idea had been forming in his mind for a while now, but he'd been uncertain how to proceed. Now he knew exactly what he wanted to do.

The bell on the microwave in the small break room of Durrant's Hardware signaled the cooking time was complete. Adam pulled his reheated meat pie out and sat down at the table. Tom walked in and smiled, pointing to the plate.

"It'll taste just as good this morning as it did last night." He moved to the fridge and removed his piece, sliding it into the oven.

Adam swallowed his first bite, nodding agreement. He'd spent his second day apart from Laura helping out at the store, unpacking shipments and stocking shelves. He liked the work, and enjoyed learning about the different kinds of merchandise Tom offered his customers.

"No customers at the moment?" The store had seen a steady stream most of the morning.

"No, but just wait until I take the first bite of my lunch and that door will buzz." Tom opened his can of soda and took a sip. "Truth is, it's getting harder to keep up with the competition. A big-box home-improvement store opened over near Sawyers Bend last year and I've seen a steady drop in business. I might move up my retirement if things keep going the way they are."

Adam didn't like to think of Tom's giving up the store. It hadn't taken long to realize that the hardware store and all the small businesses in Dover were woven into the fabric of the town. Losing Durrant's would be a blow. "Isn't there anything you can do to keep business coming in?"

"I'm going to start looking into some things. I'm a bit out of my element in that regard. I've never had to attract customers. But times are changing."

"Would you mind if I used your computer? I could do a bit of online research in the evenings, maybe come up with some ideas."

"I'd appreciate the help."

The buzzer on the front door of the store sounded, announcing a customer had walked in. Tom smiled and took one last bite of his lunch. "See? Never fails."

Adam liked the idea of helping Tom find a solution to his problem. Perhaps he could repay him in a small way for his kindness. The internet might help him with another matter he was working on, as well. A surge of excitement raced through him when he thought about what he hoped to accomplish. The thrill was familiar, but it had nothing to do with danger and everything to do with helping someone else.

Adam propped his feet up on the dashboard of Laura's truck, enjoying the familiar routine. She'd been home for a few days now and they'd settled back into their usual pattern. Up early, a quick breakfast with the Durrants, then ride with Laura to the job. They'd work until five, either on the gazebo or Handy Works projects. Then it was home, shower and supper with the Durrants. He found the predictability strangely comforting. Tom and Angie Durrant were always there, always together and always including him.

Somewhere along the way his skepticism had died, his edginess had disappeared and he'd come to look forward to the peaceful, welcoming tone of the Durrants' home. He started to feel comfortable around the couple. Almost like a member of the family. He didn't want to think about the end of his sentence. Once he left, he'd never see them again. He was simply a person passing through their lives. That thought bothered him. He wanted to be more important to them than that. He wanted to be important to Laura, as well.

The streets flying by the truck were unfamiliar to him as he rode with Laura later that morning. New directions usually meant new adventures, or more Handy Works projects. "Road trip?"

"I need to pick up some supplies from my house first. I forgot to load them this morning."

Her house? The idea made him smile. This might prove interesting. He'd wondered about her personal life. He'd almost come to the conclusion that Laura Durrant was all work and no play. All tool belt and chalk line. With her take-charge attitude, she probably lived in one of those renovated loft-type places in an old factory. Clean, sleek and no-nonsense. Everything practical and useful. No fluff for her.

He glanced out the window, surprised to see an idyllic tree-lined street. This was a part of the town he'd never seen. A quick flash of apprehension raced down his spine. "We aren't going outside of my monitor range, are we?"

"I don't think so."

Adam swallowed. "Well, I'm going to let you explain that to the cops when the alarm is triggered and they swarm the truck."

Laura slowed the truck and pulled into the driveway. Adam studied the one-story pale blue Victorian. Intricate gingerbread dripped from every angle of the porch and the gable. The broad wraparound front porch held planters filled with ferns and colorful flowers. The entire place was picture-postcard perfection.

"This is your place?"

"Yes."

He followed her toward the detached garage at the end of the drive, puzzled by this new glimpse of Laura's life. It took a few minutes to load up the boards and tie them down securely. Laura locked the garage and started back to the truck. Adam followed along, enjoying the way her chin tilted upward aggressively as she moved. He had to admit she was extremely good at her job. And extremely cute while doing it.

"Oh, no." Laura stopped in her tracks.

"What?"

"I forgot my tablet."

Adam held up his hands and leaned against the truck. "Go ahead. I'll wait right here."

She chewed her lip thoughtfully for a moment. "No. We don't know how close to the limit we are with your monitor. You'd better come inside with me."

"You have my word I won't go anywhere."

"But if something should happen and the police show up and you're not in my sight." She shook her head. "No, come in."

Laura led the way up the curved walk and across the

porch to the front door. Adam took a quick inventory of the cozy decor. Wicker chairs with flowered cushions and old metal glider painted bright aqua formed an inviting seating area at one end. Lush plants and a swing lured you to the other. It was cozy, but at odds with his impression of her.

A small bundle of fur greeted them at the door, tail wagging like a flag. "Who's this?"

"That's Drywall. Wally for short."

"Friendly little guy." Adam gently scratched the animal's neck.

Laura sifted through the stuck of items on a desk across the room, mumbling under her breath before turning her search to a pile of paper on the coffee table.

Adam glanced around the room, his ideas about Laura Durrant taking another hit. No sleek loft style here. Her home was a charming mix of traditional furniture and antiques, muted colors and lush fabrics, but all of it was very definitely feminine.

"I'll be right back."

He nodded, hooking his thumbs into the ridge of his pockets. Laura disappeared down a hallway and he took the opportunity to take a closer look at her home. A part of him knew a moment of guilt for prying into her private world, but a bigger part of him needed to satisfy his curiosity about his lovely boss.

Her home was warm and welcoming. That fit. He'd seen her display that side of herself to others. He moved farther into the room. A flat-screen television took up one wall. He wondered if she liked sports, given she had two older brothers. Dog toys were scattered around the floor, a rose-colored throw lay over one arm of the sofa. He took a step forward to see what was peeking out from under the edge. A romance novel. He smiled. So, she wasn't all drill bits and tape measures after all.

The phone rang and Adam peered around the corner into the kitchen. It rang again. "You want me to get that?"

"No."

He shrugged and moved into the kitchen. It was bright and cheery with top-of-the-line stainless steel appliances, but with a decidedly cozy, feminine appeal. A glimpse outside revealed a sunroom and just beyond a well-kept yard. Laura definitely had a domestic side.

Footsteps sounded in the hall. He turned and walked back to the foyer, arriving in time to see Laura emerge from the back of the house. She looked relieved. "Good news?"

She glanced over at him as if she'd forgotten he was there. "Yes. That was my mother on the phone. She just talked with my brother Ty in Dallas."

"How's he doing?"

"Better physically, but emotionally he's struggling. But he might be coming home in a few weeks."

"That's good to hear. I know your parents will be happy."

She nodded, wiping tears from her cheeks. "We were so scared. At first we thought he might…" She turned away.

He started toward her, eager to offer her comfort or let her cry out her worries on his shoulder. But after the other day's near kiss, she might not welcome such an intimate gesture from him. "If he's anything like the rest of the Durrants, he'll come through in good shape."

"That's what I'm praying for."

He searched for something to say to give her time to

regroup. "I like what you've done with the place. Did you restore this house?"

Laura nodded. "It didn't need much. The previous owners took good care of it." She turned and faced him, her composure once again in place. "We'd better go. We need to get those rafters replaced so we can get the roof under way."

She walked toward him and he reached over to open the door. He misjudged her movement, however, and she bumped into him. Every nerve in his body went on high alert. He remembered holding her the other day, the way she'd felt in his arms. He shoved the memory aside and stared into her warm, welcoming violet eyes. "I didn't expect you to have a home like this."

"Why?" She stood still as a statue, shifting her gaze downward, refusing to look him in the eyes again.

"I pictured you in some ultrachic loft. I hadn't taken into account your feminine side." He lifted his hand to touch the soft tendril of honey-colored hair that had escaped from her cap, but thought better of it and lowered his arm. Instead he leaned a fraction closer, inhaling her sweet tangy scent. "Don't you know what a lovely woman you are?"

She stepped back and moved past him out onto the porch.

Adam followed close behind, his mind kicking himself for getting too close again. But he couldn't seem to help himself when she was near. In fact, the only time he felt truly alive was when they were working side by side. The feeling was nothing like the adrenaline rush from one of his extreme sports. This was deeper, richer and he didn't understand it at all.

* * *

Laura snapped her cell phone closed and slipped it into her pocket. There were problems at the Conrad site. The last thing she needed was another crisis. They were popping up like weeds. This was the fourth phone call this afternoon. She was beginning to wonder if there was a conspiracy afoot to keep her from having a relaxing evening at home.

Thankfully, Shaw had everything under control, but she was the boss and the buck stopped with her. While her trip to Arkansas had been successful, it had put a strain on her budget. She didn't want to lay off any of her crew. There were a couple of prospective jobs in the works, but nothing definite yet.

Walking out into the kitchen, she glanced at Wally's empty dish. "Aw, poor little guy. You must be starved." She filled his dish and scratched lovingly behind his ears. She'd been so distracted lately, she had to resort to a daily to-do list to make sure she didn't forget anything.

Pouring a glass of tea, she carried it into the living room. Her heartbeat quickened when she looked at her front door. The memory of Adam standing there filled her mind. She'd made a huge mistake in allowing him to come into the house today. Unfortunately, she hadn't anticipated the repercussions his presence might cause. Her home had always been her sanctuary, her cozy retreat from the pressures of her job. Within these rooms she was safe to be herself, a woman instead of one of the guys. Her little Victorian house was her insulation from the world. But now, Adam had breached her private walls and seen into her heart.

She closed her eyes, rubbing them with her fingertips, attempting to erase the sight of him filling her doorway. He'd dominated the room. All that male strength in the middle of her frilly decor had been a startling and compelling contrast. She hated even more the sense of security she'd felt at his presence. He'd stood like a protector between her soft private world and the hard, real world outside. Adam's presence in her house had pointed out the one gaping hole in her life. One she wanted filled but was afraid to pursue. A husband and family.

Wally barked, jarring her from her thoughts. "It's okay, boy." She bent down and stroked his soft fur. "I'm tired and behaving like a fool."

Picking up her tablet, she managed a whole five minutes of work before she thought about Adam again. Like a video projection, his tall frame appeared in her mind's eyes. The broad shoulders, the nonchalant way he'd leaned against the door frame. The keen interest in his green eyes as he'd scanned her living room. The way he'd smiled and reached down to pet Wally with great gentleness had both surprised and touched her. She tugged Wally into her lap for a warm hug. "The way to a woman's heart is through her pet."

Thanks to his help, the gazebo should be completed in plenty of time and he could get home for his meeting with his father. Then her life could go back to normal. The prospect didn't sound as appealing as she'd thought it would. Probably because she was in serious danger of falling in love with Adam.

Her gaze drifted to the doorway again. She was afraid it was already too late. Because now, every time she walked into her living room, he'd be there. She'd slipped up and let him into her home. She couldn't afford to let him into her heart. But there might be a way to show him her gratitude. Reaching for the phone again, she dialed, hoping her dad could come through for her one more time.

The Durrant house was quiet. Peaceful. But he'd never felt so out of sorts before. He'd come to appreciate the hustle and bustle that marked the Durrants' Sunday gatherings. After that first one, he'd relaxed, convinced that the family really did get together each Sunday after church and truly enjoyed being together.

But this Sunday was different. Laura and her mother had gone to the early service, leaving him and Tom to attend the late one. Adam had enjoyed the sermon and had grown more comfortable with the citizens of Dover, who no longer stared at him like a stranger but greeted him as one of their own.

Coming home to the empty house had left him out of sorts and a bit lonely, though. Tom had jokingly encouraged him to enjoy his "free" time, explaining he had long-neglected yard work that would keep him busy most of the day. Adam tried to watch the ball game on television, but found himself restless and unable to concentrate.

Laura and her mother were giving a bridal shower for Shelby today and wouldn't be back until early evening. He missed seeing Laura flitting around the house. In fact he was beginning to miss her anytime she was out of his sight. He'd lost his heart to her from the moment she'd appeared in the doorway to his room that first day. Now he was completely lost in her beauty, her determination and her heart, and he no idea what to do about it.

Adam made his way through the Durrants' kitchen

on his way to the back porch. It had become his favorite place to relax. His gaze fell on the calendar on the wall near the door. The last day of the month mocked him. How was he going to make it to Atlanta in time for his meeting? And the way things were going, the gazebo wouldn't be finished in time for Founder's Day. Work had slowed, the materials Laura needed kept getting held up or wrong shipments delivered. They were working hard, but everything took longer than expected.

He tried to envision life without a bottomless bank account. He couldn't. For most of his adult life he'd had only one thing that he could count on—his yearly allowance. Adventures came and went. Friends drifted with the wind. But the money was constant. It gave him an identity. An anchor. When that was gone what would he have? Who would he be?

Who did he *want* to be?

Laura let herself into the front door of her parents' home. The welcoming silence and familiar smells wrapped around her like an old sweater. She walked softly through the front hall, stopping at the office door where her father was working away. "Hey, Daddy."

"Hello, Boo. How was the shower?"

"Fun. Noisy. Mom will be along in a little while. She wanted to stop by Matt's and see the kids. Where's Adam?"

"I'm not sure. He was on the back porch a while ago."

Laura made her way to the kitchen, her heartbeat quickening a little. She'd missed him today. She'd gotten used to having him nearby, ready to help or talk to. His time was winding down and she had a feeling she'd miss him even more after he left.

He was seated on the large cushioned love seat facing the backyard. He looked comfortable and relaxed. Like he belonged there. He turned and smiled when she stepped out the door.

"Welcome back. How did the big event go?"

She joined him on the love seat, drawing her feet up under her and angling her body toward him. "It was a huge success. Everyone had a great time. Shelby was overwhelmed with all the gifts. She got a lot of pretty things. Vases, candles, decorative items. Because she and Matt both had household items already, they didn't need much."

"It sure was quiet around here. I missed you."

She looked over at him, seeing the truth reflected in his eyes. "I thought you'd enjoy some alone time."

He reached out and touched her hand. "I thought so, too, but I like it better when you're around."

She looked away, searching for something say. He touched her arm. His fingers were warm and gentle. His hands were broad, strong and tanned.

"I was looking at the photos along the stairs earlier and there's a wedding picture with the name Laura Frasier underneath it. Was that your married name?"

"I took back my maiden name when he…when the divorce was final."

"What happened?"

She sighed, trying to decide how much to tell him. "I thought he was the man of my dreams. He was handsome, smart, rich and the life of the party. To a small-town girl, he was everything exciting and glamorous. But after we were married, he didn't want to settle down. He wanted to keep having a good time with his friends. A wife was a hindrance, especially when he enjoyed the company of other women more."

Adam squeezed her hand. "He was a fool."

Laura stroked her fingers over the back of his hand, enjoying the connection. It made it easier to talk. "His philandering got worse. The last straw came when I opened the newspaper and saw Ted and a woman photographed at some big social event and the caption read Mr. and Mrs. Ted Frasier." She heard Adam groan softly. "I filed for divorce the next day. We reached a settlement and I came home and bought Mr. Shuler's construction company and never looked back."

"It hurts when someone you care about betrays your trust. When you've opened your heart to them and they trample it like it's a worthless trinket."

She looked at him, but he was staring off into the distance. "You and Gail?"

"Pretty much. We'd been dating six months. I thought it was serious. Until I found out she'd been having an affair with my friend for weeks, right under my nose."

Now she understood his attitude toward the woman. He really did understand. "I'm sorry. The betrayal leaves you feeling so confused. I kept wondering what was wrong with me. Wasn't I smart enough, pretty enough? I couldn't compete with all his glamorous women." Adam suddenly placed his finger against her lips to silence her, leaning forward to gaze steadily into her eyes.

"Stop. Don't say those things. The man was an idiot. You're smart, vibrant and strong, and the most fascinating and beautiful woman I've ever met." He trailed his finger to the side of her jaw and along her chin.

Laura held her breath, gazing into his eyes, filled

with anticipation. She wanted him to kiss her. She wanted to know that sense of comfort and belonging she'd felt before.

The kitchen light came on, shattering their shadowed cocoon. Adam laughed and stood, pulling her to her feet. "It's been a long time since I've had the old porch light 'time to come inside' warning. Your father's got impeccable timing."

Adam stood at a distance the next afternoon as an elderly couple greeted Laura like a long-lost daughter. He watched her, warm affection filling his heart. He'd gotten used to her receiving this kind of reception. Everyone, friend or stranger, adored her. Laura embodied compassion and love. The sight of her never failed to steal his breath. She was capable of love so deep, so intense it would overpower a man with the sheer force of it. What would it be like to be loved like that? To be buried in love and trust so profound you'd never feel lost or alone again?

She'd stirred his conscience, his sense of right and wrong. Another part of his soul he'd long ignored. When he looked at the man in the mirror now, he didn't like what he saw. Being around Laura made him want to be a better man. A man worthy of her love. Forcing himself to inhale, he turned away, running a hand down the back of his neck. But could he ever be that kind of man? And where did he start? All he knew was that somehow, Laura Durrant had slipped behind his barriers and penetrated deep into his soul. The knowledge thrilled him and scared him at the same time.

"Adam."

He jerked his attention to her as she came toward him. "Yes?"

"We're going to replace the front steps."

"Great. That's right up my alley. Why don't you let me handle this one?"

Laura hesitated a moment, then smiled. "All right. We need to replace the screens in the back door, too. I'll take care of the work needed inside."

"Sure thing." It took him a moment to register that she was actually trusting him to work alone.

For the entire time he'd been here she had watched over him like a hawk, never allowing him more than a flicker of unsupervised time. He'd been itching for the chance to show her he wasn't a complete idiot and that he could handle a job from beginning to end. He wanted her to trust him to follow her orders, to show her that he'd learned more about carpentry than she knew.

For some strange reason, proving himself to Laura meant more to him than anything had in his entire life, and that scared him. Why was the approval of this one small-town woman so important?

He suspected he knew the answer, but he didn't want to examine that right now. At the moment, all he knew was that he wasn't about to let this opportunity get away from him.

Adam turned and smiled at the elderly man who had introduced himself as Mr. Norwood. "Well, I guess I'd better get busy."

The man harrumphed, his thick brows nearly touching as he scowled. "We don't need you, you know."

"Oh? I thought Ms. Durrant said you needed the screens fixed and the back steps replaced."

"I could do that. She didn't need to call you."

Adam nodded, wondering about the man's attitude. "You lived here long?"

"I built this house."

He stared at the slightly bent old man. "You did?"

"That's right. From the ground up. Did all the wiring and plumbing myself, too."

Adam made a quick survey of the house. With a little imagination he could see how it might have looked in its heyday. "Amazing job, Mr. Norwood."

"Call me Frank. Yeah. It took a whole year."

He moved forward and Adam was shocked at how slowly the man moved. It was obvious he was in a great deal of physical pain. He must be experiencing emotional pain, as well. Seeing the home he built with his own hands being repaired by a stranger.

"Well, maybe you could give me a hand. You're more familiar with how things work than I am."

Mr. Norwood held up his arthritis-twisted hand. "I don't have the dexterity I used to."

"No problem." Adam stepped a bit closer and lowered his voice. "See, the truth is, I'm new at this stuff. I'm surprised Ms. Durrant let me tackle this on my own. I could use your help."

Frank huffed under his breath. "Nothing to it."

An hour later, Adam stretched out his hand to Frank. "I couldn't have done it without you."

"You're a fast learner."

"Thanks. You're a good teacher." Frank stared at the front of his home.

"Been in this place forty years next week."

"Really? Is that how long you've been married?"

"Nope. Fifty-three on that end."

A few days ago he couldn't begin to imagine being with one person that long. Now all he wanted to do was to have the chance to try. "How did you do it?"

"Do what?"

"Put up with another person that long?"

Frank looked puzzled. "You've never been in love, have you, son?"

"No, guess not."

"When you do, you'll understand."

Adam shook his head. "I don't know. How can you make a woman happy for all that time?"

"You keep one hand in hers and the other in the Lord's."

The front door opened and Laura and Mrs. Norwood emerged onto the porch.

Adam and Frank joined them. "Mission accomplished." Adam smiled at Laura.

She nodded, making a quick inspection of the steps and screens. "Good work."

Adam opened his mouth to crow about his accomplishment, eagerly anticipating her praise. Finally, she'd have to admit that he wasn't as useless as she'd wanted to believe.

He caught sight of Frank Norwood out of the corner of his eye. His wife was at his side. The old man's words reverberated inside him. His pride at what he'd built, and his anger and humiliation at not being able to take care of his home, had touched something deep inside Adam. He made his choice. "Well—" he laid a hand on Frank's shoulder "—I can't take the credit. I thought I knew how to do these repairs, but I guess I'm not as smart as I thought I was. Frank had to take over and guide me every step of the way."

The old man shrugged, uncomfortable with the attention. "Oh, I don't know 'bout that. The boy's got the ability. He just needs practice, that's all."

"Did you fix all this?" Marion Norwood asked.

Adam's heart skipped a beat at the love and admiration that flooded the woman's eyes.

Frank shrugged again. "Oh, you know."

"Sweetheart, I should have listened when you said you could make the repairs." She wrapped her husband in a warm embrace.

Frank's eyes sent a message of appreciation that brought a lump to Adam's throat. Truth be told, Frank had kibitzed the entire time. While his guidance had proved valuable, he'd not actually done the work himself. It would have been easy and honest to tell everyone that he, Adam, had accomplished these small feats. Finally, he would have looked good in Laura's eyes. She would have been forced to admit that he was doing a good job at picking up carpentry and home repairs. In the past it's exactly what he would have done.

But allowing this man a chance to look like a hero in his wife's eyes one more time was worth the small sacrifice. The feeling inside his heart was like nothing he'd ever experienced before. Stepping out of the spotlight and sharing with another was foreign to him. But he liked the feeling. He liked helping. This was such a small thing. All he'd done was emphasize what Frank had done and ignore his own part in the project. Why should that make him feel almost giddy with joy? It didn't make sense.

Is this what Laura meant when she talked about giving instead of receiving? Is this what drove her desire to help others?

It confused him. Why should being less make him feel like more? He had a lot to discuss with Pastor Jim at their next meeting.

Laura stole a glance at Adam. He was staring out the truck window. She had a dozen questions she wanted to ask him, but she doubted he'd give her a straight answer. He was reluctant to talk about his personal life. But she had to know what made him behave so generously to Mr. Norwood. It went against every perception she had of him. What had changed?

She pulled the van to a stop in the Handy Works lot and Adam moved to leave. "Why did you do it?" He looked at her, puzzled. "Why did you pretend Mr. Norwood had done all the work himself?"

Adam shrugged. "He did."

"No, he didn't. I happen to know the Norwoods. They attend our church and I know Frank is incapable of doing that kind of work." She waited for him to respond, but he continued to stare out the side window.

"I know you've been anxious for me to let you work alone. So what changed?"

Adam sighed, obviously irritated with her questioning. "He was a nice old man. I wanted to help him, that's all." He turned and pinned her with his green eyes. "Isn't that what you've been preaching to me since I got here? Helping others?"

"Yes, but…"

Adam chuckled harshly. "You didn't think I had it in me."

Laura looked away. He was right and she was ashamed about that. She'd been working overtime to keep him in the nice little cubbyhole she'd assigned him to, only he refused to stay there.

"Don't worry about it. You're not completely wrong. My family wasn't big on altruism. We had more of a 'me first' kind of philosophy."

"I'm sorry." She didn't know what else to say.

"It's not your fault. Those are the cards I was dealt."

"So what changed?"

Adam smiled at her, his eyes warm. "Guess you're starting to rub off me, boss lady."

Laura replayed the conversation in her mind a dozen times that night. Something was different about Adam. Something had changed him and she wasn't arrogant enough to believe it had anything to do with her.

His kindness today had broken through her biggest concern that Adam and her ex were cut from the same cloth. Deep in her heart she'd known that wasn't true early in their relationship, but it was easier and safer to keep believing it.

Now she was forced to look at Adam Holbrook with new eyes, not ones clouded with old mistakes. In doing so, however, she had to acknowledge the fact that her attraction to Adam was much more than simple physical appreciation. There was something sweet and tender about Adam that she couldn't ignore.

She'd labeled him selfish, incapable of thinking of others. She'd been proved wrong, not only today, but every moment she'd been with him. Adam had the capacity for great compassion. He was as attracted to her as she was him, but she still couldn't forget that he was a man who craved adventure, the thrill of extreme sports. There were few thrills in Dover. They were too different. Unexpected versus predictable. Those things could never mix.

But the truth couldn't be ignored. Adam Holbrook had stolen her heart and she knew there was no hope of getting it back.

Laura rubbed her eyes and shoved aside the papers she'd been studying. She'd gone over the guidelines for restoring the gazebo, wondering how she could meet the requirements, locate the approved shingles and have them shipped to Dover all in time to complete the job by Founder's Day. None of that mattered if the forecast didn't change. Rain was predicted off and on for the next ten days. A late-season hurricane in the Gulf had skimmed the coast of Mississippi and bands of rain were spreading over the whole state.

As if that weren't bad enough, the Conrad project was behind schedule. The owner had requested last-minute changes that meant ripping out what had been done and starting over. Which in turn upped the cost and time for everyone and put her budget deeper into the hole. The situation with the Mobile job was still in limbo and her bank account was in a serious bind.

A while back, she'd considered taking a second mortgage on her house to bid on the Keller building. Her dad would have been furious, especially because there was no guarantee she'd win the auction. Now she was thinking about a loan to save her business.

She swiveled in her desk chair and looked out the window in her small office to the workshop beyond. Adam had spent the past few days doing whatever work was needed in Laura's shop. Sweeping, inventory, ordering supplies. Surprisingly, she could almost believe he enjoyed the work. Yesterday they'd spent the rainy day at the Handy Works warehouse stocking the van and inventorying materials. He'd even manned the phone one day, taking requests for assistance. Another long rainy day had sent him to her dad's store to work when she couldn't find anything else for him to do.

They were back at her shop today, Adam hovering around her cabinet maker, Jeb, as he worked. If she didn't find something for him to do they'd all go nuts.

"Adam, stop bothering Jeb and go sweep or something." She hadn't meant to sound so curt, but she was in a horrible mood. He glanced over at her and she could tell by the expression on his face that he would want an explanation.

She turned her back, but she knew the moment he came near. Her nerves always tingled in a strange way when he was close. She turned and faced him. "I'm sorry. I shouldn't have snapped at you."

"Something on your mind? I know the weather isn't doing either of us any good, but there's not much we can do about it." He looked past her to the calendar on the wall, his expression filled with understanding. "Oh. Today's the auction, isn't it?"

She didn't want to think about that, although she was touched that he'd remembered. "It's going on right now and there's nothing I can do to stop it or change it. I just hope whoever buys it will use it for something that will benefit the town."

Adam stooped down beside her chair, laying his hand on her arm. "Your dad keeps telling me the Lord makes everything work for good. Maybe He's got something planned you don't know about."

She wanted to believe that, but she also knew sometimes the Lord said no, and she was afraid this was one of those times.

Chapter Eight

The rain had moved out. For the last two days they'd been able to work and gotten nearly caught up. The new posts had been installed, a perfect match to the originals. Once they were painted no one would be able to distinguish the old from the new. But they were too far behind for her liking, and there was still a lot to do. What concerned her most was the forecast for this afternoon. More rain was on the way.

The last handrail had been secured when the first drop of moisture touched her cheek. She ignored it. It could be sap from the trees overhead. It wasn't thunder. It was a jet flying over. She frowned and pressed the nail gun against the wood. It couldn't rain. They didn't have time for rain.

The light sprinkles sent her heart into the pit of her stomach. She placed the last nail and forced a glance at the sky. If they hurried, they might be able to get this section of spindles in place before the rain shut them down. Yesterday had been a total loss to the weather. Now half of today would be lost, as well.

Suddenly the sky opened up.

"Adam!" Laura grabbed for a tarp, struggling to cover the spindles to keep them dry.

The wind tore it off. Adam appeared at her side, grabbing her by the shoulders.

"We've got to get out of here. Lightning."

"The tarp. Hurry."

He grabbed the blue plastic and wrestled it over the work table and the now-wet spindles. Laura grabbed the other end and together they managed to tie it down.

"In here."

Adam propelled her toward the interior of the gazebo where it was shielded from the torrential rain by a curtain of thick tarps on all sides. They'd put them up a few days ago so they could keep working in the drizzle.

Laura pounded a fist against one of the thick turned posts. "I can't afford this rain."

"It won't last long."

Laura shook her head. "It's going to last for the next several days. We're already so far behind we'll never finish in time for Founder's Day."

"We've got plenty of time. We'll make it."

"Not if those cypress shingles don't get here soon." She paced back and forth, arms across her chest. "I can't believe this is happening. We should be looking at painting and landscaping by now."

"What happened to the shingles that arrived yesterday?"

Laura pulled off her baseball cap and yanked the clips from her hair. "They were cypress all right, but from 1980, not 1880. I sent them back."

"But you'll find the ones you need, right?"

She nodded. "I did, but they're coming from Savannah. I'm not sure they'll get here in time." She bit her lip to keep from crying. What was wrong with her? She'd been emotional for the past few days. The least little thing choked her up.

"Hey," Adam said softly. "You'll pull this off. I have faith in you."

She wanted to cry. Where did he get off saying sweet things like that to her? "Thanks." She turned and took a seat on the bench that ran around the inside of the gazebo. "Guess we're done for today."

"We'll work harder tomorrow." Adam took a seat beside her. "I'm getting pretty good at installing those little spindles of yours. Me and the jigsaw are one."

She knew he was trying to lighten her mood and she appreciated it, but nothing would help right now. She wanted to be done in time for him to get home. But there was less than a week left and unless something miraculous happened, Adam wouldn't be leaving for Atlanta until his sentence was completed. The wind and thunder swelled. Frustrated, she stood and moved to the tarp, pulling back the edge. The rain had increased, driving down in sideways sheets, whipping the tarps around violently. A blast of cold rain drove her back. "Oh."

Adam pulled her behind him to the center of the gazebo, then hurried to retie the flapping tarp. "What were you trying to do?" he demanded, coming to her side.

She was drenched. Her shirt and light jacket were soaked through. "I thought the rain might be letting up and we could get to the truck."

Thunder roared overhead, causing the gazebo to vibrate. "I think we'll be here awhile."

Great. More time lost. She shivered as the cool air blew against her wet clothes.

"You're going to catch pneumonia." He started to

unbutton his shirt and she took a step back. Before she could move farther, he'd wrapped his shirt across her shoulders.

Its warmth still held his scent. He pulled her against him, one hand wrapped tightly across her shoulders, the other vigorously rubbing her arm to stimulate warmth. She shivered again, but not from the cold. Her hand, resting against the T-shirt that covered his broad chest, moved with the beating of his heart. She told herself to move away. But she was cold and he was warm and strong and she felt oh so safe. She dared a glance at his face. She held her breath and felt him do the same.

The air was charged with electricity. She knew what was going to happen. *Stop this. Stop it now.* But her heart had other ideas. She wanted him to kiss her. She'd wanted him to for a while now.

"Laura."

He said her name reverently and she melted against him. His lips were warm, gentle but eager and she met them the same way. His arms wrapped around her waist, crushing her to his broad chest. She was lost, sinking into the wonder and discovery of it all.

Adam ended the kiss, pulling back only far enough to caress her face with his gaze.

"So sweet." He lowered his head again, then reality struck. What was she doing? She couldn't afford to get involved with someone like Adam. They were too different. He could never stay put and she could never pull up roots and leave.

Fear surged upward into her chest and she pushed Adam away, backing up until she bumped against a post.

Adam stared at her, and the look in his eyes brought

her to tears. Behind the surprise was a pain and sadness so profound she had to look away. A second realization hit her then. This wasn't about Ted or Adam. This was all about her. This was all about her fear of being hurt. More specifically her distrust of God's plans for her life.

"Adam," her voice quivered.

He shook his head, a tight smile on his face. "No need to explain. I understand. I stepped over the line. It'll never happen again. Promise." He turned and moved to the other side of the gazebo and untied the flap.

The rain had eased up. The storm had passed.

"We can make that run to the truck now." Adam kept his back to her.

She pulled his shirt from her shoulders and handed it to him as she passed, careful not to let her hand touch his. Safely in the truck, she tried to ignore the heavy tension that hovered between them as they drove to her parents' house. Adam got out, gave a salute and hurried to the porch. She watched him disappear inside, fighting the need to cry. She should have stopped the kiss. It had only confirmed what she'd suspected. She was in love in Adam Holbrook.

The awful truth was it was one-sided. Oh, he was attracted, she knew that, but there was no future for them. No future for the gazebo, no hope for Keller building and no hope of getting Adam home in time to meet with his father.

Once safely inside her home, she curled up on the sofa and gave in to the tears. This story couldn't have a happy ending because in just a few days, Adam would lose everything and it would be all her fault.

Chapter Nine

Laura stole a quick glance at her passenger. Adam smiled and stretched his body into a more comfortable position. The generous truck cab began to shrink. She was acutely aware of his every move, every breath. Nervousness loosened her tongue. "I'm really hopeful this place will pan out. It's a turn-of-the-century Italianate Victorian just outside town. I need to see if it's worth restoring. Supposedly most of the historic aspects are intact, but I'm not sure about the bones of the place. I want to make a quick check before I hire engineers to inspect it."

"Sounds interesting."

A short time later they pulled into the drive of an old brick mansion. Laura stopped near the carriage house in the back. All concerns about Adam vanished when she saw the old home. Her imagination caught fire with possibilities. It was one of the original homes in Dover and the thought of bringing it back to its former glory excited her.

Laura dug out the key the Realtor had given her and unlocked the weathered side door. They entered through a small vestibule into the sunroom. Three walls of windows rose upward twelve feet, ending in an arched roof made of glass. Laura smiled, her mind filing with vignettes of using the room on a rainy day to read a book, or curling up on a sweet Sunday afternoon with someone she loved. "Isn't it a wonderful old place?" She trailed her hand over the small panes of glass in the windows.

Adam nodded, his attention focused on the woodwork inside the next room. "This is amazing. I've never seen anything like this craftsmanship."

Laura wandered past him deeper into the house. It had fourteen-foot ceilings, one-of-a-kind fireplace surrounds and several stained-glass windows. "Now you can see why I love to work on these old places."

Adam stooped down to examine the tile surround on a fireplace. "What is this stuff?"

Laura came and leaned over him. "Porcelain relief tiles. It was a sign of wealth at the time to have them designed specifically for each room." Adam turned his head and smiled up at her. Her heart skipped a beat and she inhaled abruptly, drawing his woodsy scent deep into her lungs. Her cheeks flushed and her mind replayed their kiss.

Straightening, she turned away, but Adam was right beside her. The air in the old home became oppressive and muggy. Thanks to the hurricane, it was an unusually humid October day in Mississippi. Of course the house would feel stuffy and uncomfortable. It had nothing to do with Adam being so close beside her. So why was her heart pounding and her mind replaying their kiss like some crazy video loop?

She started toward the back of the house to inspect

the kitchen, acutely aware of Adam's every move, every breath. She glanced at him to see if he suspected her discomfort. His green eyes met hers and she knew without a doubt that he was remembering the kiss, as well. She stopped in the middle of the kitchen, intending to comment on its sorry state, when Adam touched her arm. She jumped.

"So what do you think?"

She gulped down the lump in her throat. Was he asking her about that kiss? She'd hoped he'd let it go and forget the entire incident. She looked into his eyes. He stood so close she could see the rise and fall of his broad chest, the day-old stubble on his strong chin. He made her feel so small and feminine. "About what?" she finally managed to ask.

He smiled again. "The house. Can it be saved?"

"Oh. I don't know yet." She turned and hurried through the kitchen and into another room, eager to put distance between them.

Her attraction was getting out of hand. Her pulse raced and her heart pounded in her chest every time she thought about him, but she didn't want him to see how she felt. It would be too humiliating. Her only hope was that when he was gone, she'd get over it and move on with her life. But move on to what?

They wandered through the rooms, but she was unable to make any real assessments. All she could think of was Adam. If he hadn't kissed her, it would have been easier to deal with him. But he had and she couldn't erase it from her mind. Worse still, she found she didn't want to.

She turned to move to the next room and came face-to-face with Adam again. He didn't move. His green eyes caressed her. Her lungs refused to work. Her heart pounded. The air became charged with electricity just like before. He wanted to kiss her again and Lord forgive her, she wanted that, too.

But the idea terrified her. She found her voice and stepped away from him. "I want to go upstairs. I need to see what condition it's in."

The stale air made Adam even more aware of Laura's scent. The fresh, citrus fragrance that always surrounded her. He exhaled slowly, bracing himself against the feelings her nearness caused. Maybe a little space between him and Laura would be a good thing. "I'll wait down here. You go ahead."

Laura studied him a moment, her violet eyes inquisitive. Did she see his growing attraction on his face? Could she feel the way his heart pounded whenever she was near?

She shrugged. "Suit yourself. I'll be right back."

Adam ran a hand along the back of his neck as he heard Laura tromping up the stairs. He had to do something about these feelings he was having. It wasn't right. Laura was his boss. Her father was his jailer. Falling in love with his daughter amounted to betraying Tom's trust.

He should never have kissed her. He should have tried harder to resist, but she'd looked so small and helpless, her clothes and hair damp from the rain. He'd been overcome with an intense need to comfort her, wrap her in his arms and ward off the cold. But once there, he'd been powerless to deny the question that had plagued him from the moment he'd met her: What would it be like to kiss her?

For a fleeting second, he'd thought she'd returned the kiss, that she'd welcomed it, but the truth had hit him when she pushed him away. She'd never care about someone like him. He didn't belong in her world.

The rejection had been a cold slap in the face, but one he needed. He moved through the old house, staring at the large stained-glass window in the entryway, only partially aware of what he was looking at. He thought about Laura day and night. He couldn't sleep anymore. Was this love? If so, he'd never felt anything like it in his life. None of his relationships had ever produced this need to protect or the driving desire to know everything about her.

Love. What did he know about love? Laura was love personified. A woman like that needed someone who could love her the way she deserved to be loved. He was a cripple in that regard. He closed his eyes. What did he have to offer her?

A loud crash thundered through the stale air.

Upstairs. Laura.

Adam turned and ran for the stairs, taking them three at a time. "Laura!" He heard a low moan and hurried down the hall, searching two rooms before he found her in the back bedroom.

"In here!"

She sounded breathless. He stepped into the room and froze. For the first time in years, Adam Holbrook sincerely prayed. She was half sitting, half lying on the floor. Her right leg disappeared into the floorboards. Her violet eyes were wide with fear. Adam pushed aside his intense fear, unwilling to let her see his own terror. "Laura?" He started across the wood floor.

"Stop." She shook her head. "The floor up here is rotten in spots. You could fall through, too."

He stopped, visually inspecting the floorboards. There was a definite discoloration near Laura, but the wood in the rest of the room was a uniform color and appeared solid. "It's okay. I think the only bad spot is where you are." Slowly he started forward, testing the floor strength with each step. He stooped down beside her, holding her gaze and trying to stay calm. "Where are you hurt?"

Tears glistened in her eyes. "My arm. My leg." She tried to pull it out of the floor but yelped in pain.

"Don't move." Slowly he shifted his position, sitting on the floor and scooting as close as he could without getting too close to the rotten flooring. His stomach clenched when he saw the blood on her arm and the angle at which her leg disappeared into the floor. He forced a smile. "How did you end up in this situation, Boo?" He brushed plaster dust from her hair and glanced upward. A chunk of the ceiling had fallen, the biggest piece missing her by only a few inches.

"I wasn't paying attention. I wanted to see how damaged the window frames were and I didn't notice the rotten floor. When I fell through it must have jarred the ceiling plaster loose and some of it hit my arm."

"Can you move your leg? Can I pull you out of there?"

Slipping his arms under hers, he lifted gently.

"Ow." Tears spilled over from her eyes. "It hurts."

"It's okay. Lie still. I don't want to move you." He reached for the phone in his back pocket only to remember he had no such privilege. "Where's your phone? We need to get someone here to help you."

"My holster."

Adam carefully slipped his fingers along her waist until he located the small pouch that held her phone. He moved gingerly, trying not to cause any movement to the arm that lay limp and bleeding at her side or the leg trapped in the broken floorboards. She whimpered as he pulled it out and he kicked himself for being such a clumsy oaf.

He made the call, then turned his attention back to Laura. She lay half on her side, half on her back. Her hard hat had been knocked off and rolled across the floor. He had to do something to make her more comfortable, but he didn't dare move her for fear of causing more injuries.

"The ambulance should be here in a few minutes."

"I'm not hurt that bad, really." She lifted her injured arm to get a better look. "Oh, great. It's going to be hard to swing a hammer for a while." She lowered her arm, wincing in pain.

"That's why you have me. Try not to move."

"I'm fine. I just feel stupid."

Adam sat on the floor behind her, scooting as close as possible so she could rest her upper body against his chest. "Don't talk. Rest. You don't want to take any chances."

She nodded and closed her eyes. "Sorry."

"For what?"

"I should have taken you back before we drove out here. I just realized that we are probably out of your range. You'll be in trouble."

How typical of her to think of others before herself. "Won't be the first time."

She nodded, then relaxed. "My leg is throbbing."

"Hang on. Help is on the way." Adam reached out and gently brushed a dust-coated tendril of hair from her forehead. Laura opened her eyes and he let himself be drawn into the lovely depths. For a fleeting second he thought he saw behind the pain and the worry, and his heart skipped a beat.

Was it possible that she cared for him a little? Hope filled his soul. He smiled and cradled her face in the palm of his hand. "I shouldn't have let you come up here alone."

"I knew better. I can be a bit bullheaded at times."

"Ya think?"

She laughed, gasping. "My arm."

"Shh. Take it easy." He stroked her head, reveling in the feel of her close against his chest, wishing he could cradle her in his arms, but moving her risked doing more damage. "You know, I thought you looked good with sawdust all over you, but you're even pretty when you're covered with plaster dust." Why had he said that? The smile on his face froze.

Laura held his gaze. "You have terrible taste in women."

"No. For the first time in my life I think I finally got it right." Adam drew his thumb and forefinger down the slope of her face, gently caressing her chin. "You're the most amazing woman I've ever known."

Laura blushed, averting her gaze. "Amazingly stupid. This was an rookie mistake."

"I know about those."

She smiled up at him in understanding and his heart fell into her lap. Whatever the outcome of this little adventure, he knew Laura Durrant would hold a part of him in her small hand forever.

Laura closed her eyes and leaned back against his chest. "Talk to me."

He welcomed the suggestion. Talking was better than dwelling on any of the thoughts rushing through his head at the moment. "Any particular subject?"

"You."

"What about me?"

"Tell me your dreams."

He'd sooner have her ask to cut off a limb, but he'd learned that Laura valued truth and this wasn't the time to embellish or brush her off. "Promise you won't tell anyone? I have a reputation, you know." He tried to keep his tone playful. She nodded.

His stomach knotted. His whole life had been about keeping his feelings hidden, even from himself, yet he was prepared to open his heart to her. "I want a family someday."

She stiffened slightly in his arms, then relaxed. He waited, uncertain whether to go on.

"You do?"

"Surprising, huh? I told you I grew up alone. No child should grow up that way. I'd like to live a normal life, raise a family. Like—" he hesitated "—like your family."

"You want children?"

Adam winced at the question. He knew she was doubtful of his qualifications. He couldn't blame her. "Several, but I don't think it'll ever happen. It's only a dream."

"Why do you say that?"

"I'd make a lousy father. My only role model was my own father. All I know is what doesn't work when it comes to raising kids, not what does."

Laura was silent a long while and Adam knew she was trying to make sense of his pipe dream. It didn't take a genius to see he wasn't cut out for family life.

"Are you sure that would be a big enough adventure for you? Normal life can get boring and monotonous."

Adam wrapped his arms a little tighter around her. Not with her. Life with her would be pure joy. "With the right person, it would be the biggest adventure ever."

Sirens wailed from outside. "The cavalry has arrived." He held her a bit closer as relief washed through him.

"Dover Police."

He'd been expecting the paramedics, but he'd take what he could get. "Up here!"

Officer Barnes entered the room, hand on holster. He eased up when he saw the situation. "What happened?"

Laura frowned. "Isn't it obvious?"

"You're out of your boundary, Holbrook."

He returned the officer's hard stare with one of his own. "I had a good reason."

"The law doesn't recognize reasons."

"I couldn't leave her."

Footsteps sounded on the stairs. The paramedics had arrived.

Laura held up her good arm. "Tell them to be careful. This floor isn't safe. It probably can't hold all of you. If it collapsed under me, it's probably rotten all the way through."

Officer Barnes motioned to the medical team to stay put at the top of the stairs. "Holbrook, you come down with me. We'll go back to the jail. These men can take care of Laura."

"No, I want to make sure she's all right."

Laura touched his arm. "Go. I'm in good hands. I don't want you to get into trouble. Please. Call my dad. He'll help you."

Adam touched her face one more time. He stood and walked to the top of the stairs. One last glance and he followed the officer down as the medics made their way to Laura.

In the squad car, Adam chewed the inside of his mouth anxiously. "Where will they take her?"

"Depends on how badly she's hurt."

"Can you call them and find out?"

"Not now. Let them do their job. I told them to give me a report as soon as possible. I promise, I'll let you know."

"Thanks."

A new concern reared its head as they drove past the town square. "What about the finishing the gazebo?"

Officer Barnes glanced at him. "Since when do you care about that?"

"It has to be done on time. It's important to her, to the town."

Barnes snickered. "Finally figured that out, huh?"

Two hours later, Adam walked from the jail with Tom Durrant at his side. Tom had assured him Laura would be all right, but still his gut clenched with the thought of her suffering. He wouldn't rest until he knew for certain.

"You're sure it's not serious?"

"Adam, she's my baby girl. Believe me, I'm more concerned than you are. Well, almost anyway."

He slid into the passenger seat of Tom's car. "How is she?"

"Nothing serious, but she'll be out of commission

for a while. Minor cuts to her arm, but it's sprained. Same for the leg."

"Thank God." Adam resting his head against the back of the seat. Relief surged through him.

"She was lucky. Bill, the paramedic, said that section of the floor was so bad she could have gone through to the floor below. That would have been a fourteen-foot fall. Good thing she's small and doesn't weigh much."

Adam echoed her father's sentiments. When he thought about what could have happened to her, his blood chilled. He'd been grateful that his own weight hadn't made matters worse.

"Praise God you were there with her, Adam. If she'd been alone…"

"I know." He remembered how small and fragile she'd felt in his arms. He'd wanted to keep her there forever. He'd gladly give up all he had to make that happen.

It hit him like a thunderbolt with a force that left him breathless and shaking. He loved Laura Durrant. He loved her wholly, completely, irrevocably. How had it happened? His heart was so filled with joy. He looked down at his hands in wonder. What a feeling! He'd never experienced anything like it in his life. He turned his face toward the passenger window, unwilling to let Tom see the emotions in his face.

He'd walked the edge of life and death, teetered on the rim of disaster and thumbed his nose in glee as he walked away unscathed. None of that could begin to compare to loving Laura. His heart raced in his chest, making it hard to breathe. Is this what it was like for everyone? Old Mr. Norwood? Did Laura's brother Matt feel like this for Shelby? It was agony. It knotted his gut, left him confused and hurting, but at the same time filled him with an unspeakable happiness. He willed himself to calm down, to retreat into the nice gray existence where he'd spent most of his life. He closed his eyes. *Lord, I don't know what to do with this feeling.*

Mr. Norwood had told him to put one hand in God's and the other in the hand of the woman he loved. That wasn't an option for him. Laura was sunlight and warmth. He was cold and empty. No, that wasn't true any longer. His love for her had chased the cold away and filled the emptiness with love for her.

The outlook for him, however, was bleak. He would do anything for her. Sacrifice all he had, but the one thing she needed most was the one thing he didn't have. He had no idea how to love her.

Laura eased down onto her sofa and turned sideways so she could prop her sprained leg on a pillow. She ached everywhere. Her head throbbed. Wally jumped up on the sofa, jarring her sore leg. She resettled him in her lap, stroking his fur and feeling some of her tension ease.

She wanted to talk to Adam, to thank him for his help. She'd replayed the accident a million times in her head over the past few hours. He'd been so tender, so sweet and thoughtful as they'd waited for the EMTs. Without him there she would have panicked. She might have been stranded there for hours before anyone knew she was missing. She reached up and touched her cheek, remembering his confession about his dreams. His answer, however, quickened her heart. He wanted a family. Had he meant it or had he been saying the things she wanted to hear to make her feel better?

There were depths to him that she'd suspected but

had denied. His kind, tender consideration at the house had further endeared him to her. But she was still afraid to take the last step. She'd seen her brother Matt struggle to love again. He'd finally admitted his fear and allowed himself to love Shelby again. She wasn't as brave or as strong as Matt.

Besides, their relationship was based on a thirty-day sentence. A forced association, not by choice. They each had a goal and those weren't compatible. No matter how she felt, Adam would be leaving soon.

A knock on the door brought a groan from her throat. She'd just gotten comfortable. She scooted around and stood, shooing Wally out of the way. She didn't need to fall over the dog right now.

The silhouette on the other side of the leaded glass door made her think her dad had returned. She opened the door and froze. "Adam, what are you doing here? How did you get here?"

He held her gaze. "I talked your dad into stopping by so I could see for myself you were all right. He's waiting for me. I can't stay long." He came toward her, taking her hands in his and inspecting her closely from the wrap on her arm to the small bandage covering the gash on her neck.

She looked into his eyes and forgot to breathe. The profound concern she saw reflected there stunned her. He cared about her. Truly cared.

"Are you sure you're all right?" His voice was thick with anxiety.

Laura nodded. "Sprained wrist, a couple of stitches in the arm." She glanced down at her leg. "I strained the muscles in my knee and hip. Nothing life-threatening, but uncomfortable."

"Good." His finger stroked the back of her hand, sending tingles along her spine.

"Thank you for staying with me."

"I'm glad I was there."

"Me, too."

She wanted to tell him how much she cared for him, but the words wouldn't come. She searched for something to end the awkward silence. Adam saved the moment.

"I never realized before how dangerous your job could be. Promise me you'll be careful when you go into these old places. You could be seriously hurt."

A shiver coursed through her at the warm concern in his deep voice. It took all her effort to extract her hand from his. "I will."

"No work for a while, huh?"

She shook her head. "But I've got stacks of paperwork and at least a half-dozen plans to go over. As far as the gazebo is concerned, I've asked Shaw to work with you on the gazebo if you want to, weather permitting."

Adam smiled. "Good. I want to keep working. Any word on when this rain will let up?"

She shook her head, painfully aware of what they both had to lose if the rain continued. "I'm sorry."

"Not your fault. You don't control the weather."

"I know, but I was trying to get it all done so you could—"

Adam held up his hand. "I know and I appreciate it, but some things aren't meant to be."

"Don't give up." She reached out and touched his arm. "We can still get the repairs done in time for you to get home for your meeting."

Adam laid his hand on hers. "I'm not giving up. I'm

trying to be realistic. In a few days I may lose everything."

"No." It surprised her much she wanted to make the
deadline for his sake. "I'll find a way to get the gazebo
done. If the shingles arrive on time we can do a lot of
work under the tarps whether it's raining or not."

Adam shook his head. "Your dad told me things happen for a reason and that they always work for good."

"I believe they do, but..."

"Then maybe that's what's happening now." A car
horn sounded from outside. "I've got to go." He kissed
her forehead, smiling into her eyes.

Laura sucked in a shaky breath. "Okay." He walked
out the door, leaving her with a new ache to add to the
others.

Chapter Ten

Rain overflowed the gutters, creating a curtain of water along the front of the Durrants' large porch and casting a fine mist several feet inside the railing. Adam ignored the growing dampness on his clothes. "Please, Lord, you calmed the sea, calm this storm so I can complete this job for her sake. For the town's sake."

He rubbed the bridge of his nose, trying to sort through the emotional chaos of this day. His stomach knotted whenever he thought about what could have happened to Laura in that old house if he hadn't been there. He'd thanked the Lord a dozen times for keeping her from serious harm.

The accident had torn open his heart, revealing his love. The emotions at work inside him now were like nothing he'd ever known. They churned with a force that no jump from a cliff, no two-hundred-mile-per-hour rush down a speedway could match. Those had been hollow sensations. Mere kiddie rides in a park. None of those thrills could compare with the love he felt for Laura. But as much as he loved Laura, as much as he'd come to love Dover, he wasn't dumb enough to think he had a future here.

"Adam, everything okay out here?"

He turned at the sound of Tom's voice.

"Something eating at you?"

"No. Yes." Adam ran a hand down the back of his neck.

"Which is it?"

He'd come to value the man's advice and his friendship, and he needed it now more than ever. He took a deep breath, gauging his words. "Have you ever wanted something so badly, but knew you had no hope of ever getting it?"

Tom nodded thoughtfully. "What is it you want?"

Adam crossed his arms over his chest, struggling with the decision to tell him about his feelings or to keep them to himself. The choice was simple. He needed to understand the intensity of what he was feeling. "Laura."

He looked over at Tom, the knowing smile on his face telling Adam his revelation had come as no surprise to her father. "How did you know?"

"I know the look in my little girl's eyes. And there's a certain—" he tilted his head slightly "—energy when you're in the same room together."

Great. Could Laura see his feelings as easily? He'd hoped to keep it from her. "I'm in love with her, but I didn't expect it to feel like this."

"Maybe that's because you've never been truly in love before."

Adam shook his head and sat down on the porch swing. "I've jumped out of helicopters. I've swum with sharks and risked my life more times than I can remember. None of that compares to how I feel about her."

"Love is a powerful emotion." Tom took a seat in one of the wicker chairs.

Powerful? More like overwhelming. The pain of it pressed on his chest like being forty fathoms beneath the sea.

"Does she know how you feel?"

"I don't think so." Adam shrugged. "Maybe. She knows I have feelings for her, but I don't think she knows how much."

"You going to tell her?"

"No."

Tom raised his eyebrows. "What if she feels the same?"

"No, that's impossible."

"With God all things are possible."

"It would never work. We're too different."

"How do you know? Have you talked with her about it?"

"No."

"Why not?"

Wasn't it obvious to Tom of all people? "Because I'm a man under house arrest. And she's my boss."

"I think you've moved beyond that, don't you?"

"I have no future. Nothing to offer."

"Not true. Your future may be uncertain at the moment, but you have a great deal to offer, Adam." Tom rested his forearms on his knees, leaning closer. "I know you think in keeping silent you're sparing her heart, but you're only hurting her more."

"What do I do?"

"Tell her the truth. Admit your feelings and your

concerns and let her decide what she wants to do with that information. Then work it out together. The biggest mistake people make is thinking we know what's best for someone else. It takes two to build and maintain a relationship. Talking. Compromising. Listening to what the other wants and needs. It's worked for me and her mother for over forty years now."

Adam stood and paced. "It's all so messed up. One minute I want to hold her like she's a fragile piece of glass. The next I want to lay down my life to keep her safe. If this is love, I don't want it." He realized who he was talking to and stood and walked to the edge of the porch, putting some distance between them. "Sorry. You're her father. I shouldn't be telling you this stuff."

"I'm the perfect one to tell. I've loved her more and longer than you. And I want her to be happy."

"That's what I want, too, but I'm not sure I'm the one to do that. How do I know it's love and not just some weird fascination that'll fade away?"

Tom rose and came to his side, laying a hand on his shoulder. "When your first and constant desire is for her happiness and not your own, that's love. Then you give it all over to the Lord. The love. The fears. The expectations and doubts. He'll work it all out."

Adam remained on the porch a long while, thinking about Tom's advice. The rain had died down and his hope had started to rise. Tom had put so many things into perspective. He owed the man so much. He'd never be able to repay his kindness, his friendship or his guidance. He felt at peace. His soul was right with God. His body was strong from physical labor and his heart was overflowing with love.

Tom had counseled him to trust the Lord to work

things out between him and Laura. All that he really wanted was for Laura to achieve her goal—the gazebo done for the festival. Nothing else mattered.

Reporting to work the next morning didn't feel right. McKinney had picked him up and driven to the gazebo in half the time Laura took. Without Laura working at his side, he truly felt as if he were serving a sentence. He'd welcomed the chance to take on more responsibility to help her, but now that he was actually faced with the reality, he didn't like the feeling. The gazebo was Laura's pride and joy. To work on it without her seemed disrespectful.

Adam shot the last nail into the last bench seat and straightened. The clouds were casting a dreary pall on the day. It suited his mood. Still, when he looked at the work he'd accomplished so far, he knew a sense of satisfaction. If someone would have told him a few weeks ago that he'd enjoy rebuilding an old gazebo, he'd have called them crazy.

"Not bad. You may have a future in this."

"Thanks." Adam stood, taking the statement from McKinney at face value. They'd barely spoken to each other all day except to exchange information or instruction. "I may need you as a reference soon."

"What?" Shaw frowned.

"Never mind." Adam hadn't made up his mind about the man yet. He couldn't get a solid read on him. He worked quietly, totally focused on his task. He hadn't displayed any desire to talk or joke or even complain. Adam had decided it was a personal grudge against him. One part irritation that he had to help the guy who damaged the gazebo, and one part desire to stand in the gap as protector for Laura.

He had a lot to think about, mainly what he would do when his deadline passed tomorrow and he wasn't in Atlanta. There were other things on his mind, too. "Have you heard from Laura this afternoon?" Today was the first time since arriving in Dover that he missed his cell phone. He wished he could call and check on her, hear her voice.

"Yeah," Shaw replied.

"How's she doing?"

Shaw studied him a moment before answering. "Fine." Shaw dropped his hammer into the loop on his tool belt and set his hands on his hips, pinning him with steely navy blue eyes. "I've worked for a lot of contractors in the South. LC is the best."

"I'm not surprised. She can be scary." Adam chuckled, attempting to lighten what he knew was a looming confrontation.

"She's tough, but she's fair and she's got a heart for people. That's what makes the difference."

"I agree."

"Look, Holbrook, I'm going to put it right out there so there's no misunderstanding. LC is a special lady. She deserves someone just as special."

Adam set his jaw. "You volunteering?" Something dark and ominous passed across the foreman's eyes. He straightened and took a step toward him.

"I work for her. She's a friend. I don't want to see her make a mistake she'll regret for the rest of her life."

"I agree." *Someone better than you.* Shaw McKinney hadn't said the words, but Adam had heard them nonetheless. Someone who could love her the way she deserved to be loved. He had no clue how to do that. He loved her with everything he had, but it could never be enough. She needed someone who understood love, how to give it and how to receive it. He couldn't risk letting her down. She'd already been hurt too much.

He turned his attention back to his work, trying to ignore the knife in his heart. McKinney was right. It was time to be realistic. His sentence was almost up. His future likely gone. He wasn't cut out for family life. All he wanted right now was to give her the thing she wanted most. He'd finish her little gazebo, then be on his way.

"Please, Lord, make the rain stop." Laura allowed the curtain at her kitchen window to drop back into place and reached for her cup of coffee. Another day of on-and-off showers. Thankfully, the forecast for tomorrow and through the weekend was good, so the Founder's Day activities would go on as planned under sunny skies and pleasant temperatures. But it might happen without the historic gazebo.

The old cedar shingles should have been delivered to the job site around noon, but that left only this afternoon and tomorrow morning to get the roof finished. And the cupola still had to be installed. As much as she hated failing in her job to restore the gazebo, she hated failing Adam more. His deadline had come and gone. His world had changed forever. She'd wanted so much for him to make it home. It was important to him and he was important to her. Very important.

Swallowing the lump in her throat, she struggled with her newly discovered feelings. She loved Adam Holbrook. She'd spent the whole night trying to pinpoint the moment she'd lost the fight and fallen in love with him. She'd barely slept. Her head knew full well he was the wrong man to love. He was a rootless adventurer, she was a stay-at-home family kind of girl. But her heart saw a man alone, who yearned for roots and a family. A man who'd reconnected with his faith, who had met a challenge with determination. A man who had learned the inner satisfaction and peace of service to others. A man worthy of love.

Her heart wanted him to stay here. She wanted him to be part of her life in Dover, but she wasn't a fool. She'd tried fitting into Ted's life and was met with disaster. She couldn't ask Adam to try to fit into a world he knew nothing about.

Laura exhaled in frustration and went in search of her keys. She couldn't stay in this house another minute. She had to know how things were going at the gazebo. She had to know how Adam was doing and see for herself he was all right. A few minutes later she pulled her truck to the curb in front of the gazebo and turned off the engine. Her gaze searched out Adam. He was bent over the workbench. His posture spoke of his intense concentration and her heart swelled with pride. And love.

He didn't look up as she came near. She noticed the bundles of shingles, a few of which were already placed on the scaffold. Finally, the end of the project was in sight. Adam turned and stared at her, his gaze cool and indifferent.

"What are you doing here? You're not supposed to be driving yet."

"I'm fine. I wanted to make sure the shingles arrived."

"There're here. Go home."

Laura stared at his stiff jaw, the tense angle of his shoulders. "What about you? I wanted to know how you were."

"I'm working."

"I meant the meeting. Your deadline, I wanted to tell you…"

"It's done. Go home."

Something was wrong. He must be devastated and trying to hide it from her. She reached out and touched his arm. He jerked it away, sending a dark glare in her direction.

"Go home, Laura. I have work to do."

She swallowed her hurt feelings, trying to find her boss facade to duck behind for protection. "You've done more than necessary, Adam." A light rain started to fall and she hurried into the gazebo to keep dry. "It's raining."

Adam started toward the scaffold with the nail gun. "So? Is there a reason why the shingles can't be put on during the rain? Will they melt or something?"

"No, but it's dangerous. The roof will be slippery."

Adam climbed up onto the scaffold. "It has to be done. You can't. That leaves me."

Laura shook her head. "At least wait until the rain stops." He stared down at her, his green eyes dark and angry.

"Don't you think I can do this?"

"Yes, of course, but…"

"Then go home and leave me be."

Tears sprung in her eyes. Her heart burned. She started out of the gazebo, noticing the rain had stopped as suddenly as it had started. Shaw took her arm as she came down the steps, steering her toward the fence. He unhooked it.

"We've got this, boss. Go on. Get out of here."

"I just want to help. This is my responsibility after all."

"We'll be done by noon tomorrow. You have my word."

"He shouldn't be up on that slippery roof. You know how dangerous that is."

Shaw leaned in, his dark blue eyes capturing her full attention. "You heard the man. Go home. Let him do what he has to do."

The fist in Adam's gut had grown larger every minute since Laura had left. He'd watched her drive away, knowing he'd hurt her, and knowing it was for her own good. She'd understand one day. He needed to finish this job on his own. Having the gazebo done in time for the festival was Laura's dream. And he was determined to make it happen.

He was officially cut off. He'd tried to call his father several times this week and had left messages but gotten no response. That bothered him more than the loss of his trust fund. He'd come to understand that he shared equal guilt in the strained relationship with his father. He wanted to go home and try and correct that if possible. Losing Laura, however, was another matter entirely. He placed the nail gun against the old cedar and pulled the trigger. He'd prayed all night, asking for some reason why the Lord had revealed a love for Laura only to deny him the fulfillment of that love.

He placed another shingle and nailed it in place. The gazebo was important to her, to the town. In the past week, signs for the festival had started popping up everywhere. Huge banners on the light posts, signs in windows, flyers. All of which was driving him to complete his task on time.

He'd found himself triple checking his measurements, taking extra care with his work. Somewhere he'd begun to compare the old craftsmanship in the gazebo with the work he was doing alongside of it. Because of Laura's love and dedication, the wood in the repaired section was nearly a perfect match for the old. The old meshing with the new.

It could be a statement about his own life. The old Adam, consumed with self, running after something that would give him a reason to exist. The man he was today was so very different. His first thoughts now were for Laura and what would make her happy. According to Tom, that was love. But theirs was a love with no future. Wasn't it?

Laura curled up in the corner of her sofa, cradling the phone to her ear, while wiping tears from her eyes. "Mom, he lost everything today. I tried so hard to finish early. It's all my fault."

"Nonsense. You did everything you could. I'm sure Adam understands that."

"I don't know. He's changed. Something happened. We were getting close, then today he acted as if he didn't want me anywhere near him."

"He was probably upset, Laura. This must have been a difficult day for him."

"I guess. Or maybe he's just now showing his true colors. He was probably paying attention to me hoping to get out of his sentence early. Then when I couldn't come through for him, he realized there was no reason to play nice."

"Laura, do you really believe that?"

"No." She sagged deeper into her sofa, hugging Wally to her side for comfort. "But he was so distant, so angry today. It scared me. I don't understand."

"He's been like that here, too. Ever since your accident at the house. I assumed he was worried about you, but he's been withdrawing more each day. I asked your dad about it, but he wouldn't tell me anything."

Laura wiped fresh tears from her cheeks. "He'll be leaving in a few days. His sentence is over on Friday."

"And you were hoping he'd stay?"

She nodded. "Stupid, huh? He told me from the beginning that he could never live in a place like Dover."

"Oh, I don't know. I think he's come to like our little town."

"Not enough. He's turned all his energy toward finishing the gazebo. He's working like a madman. Even Shaw made me leave him alone. It scares me."

"He knows how much the gazebo means to you, sweetheart. He's probably wanting to get it done in time. That's all."

Was that it? Was his fierce determination because of the festival or because it was important to her?

"Do you love him?"

Laura froze. She'd only acknowledged her feelings last night. How had her mother guessed? No use in pretending. Her mother could read her like a book. "Yes. Crazy, isn't it? I made a big mistake with a rich guy once before. You'd think I'd learned my lesson."

"Adam isn't Ted, Laura. Anyone can see that. Yes, you made a mistake before, but I don't think loving

Adam would be one. I don't know Adam well, but he strikes me as a man who would find strong emotions very difficult to process. Particularly those of loss and love. Maybe he's afraid he'll fail you."

"I don't care if the gazebo is done or not. The festival will go on regardless."

"I'm not talking about the gazebo. Maybe he's afraid he can't be the man you need him to be."

Was that possible? None of it made sense. There were so many things to sort through and so little time left to do that. Adam would be gone from her life in a matter of days. "What do I do, Mom?"

"Tell him how you feel. You might not get another chance."

Laura thought about her mother's advice as she tried to sleep that night. Should she tell Adam she loved him? What if he rejected her? But on the other hand, what if she was missing her chance at happiness because she was hanging too tightly on to her fear of the past? She'd seen enough with her own eyes to know that Adam was a changed man. She also knew he was scared. Scared of his feelings and his emotions.

Lord, I need some wisdom and clarity. I don't know what to do.

Adam cut the wire binding on the shingles and started the last row. Three hours later, he stood back and scanned the completed roof critically. Officially, his work was done. All that remained was to replace the cupola. The crane would be here in a few hours to lift the large decorative cap into place.

Down below, he could hear Shaw working diligently on all the detailed finish work. He'd made it. The gazebo would be ready in time for the Founder's Day celebration on Saturday. The painters would come first thing in the morning along with the landscapers. By the end of the day tomorrow, everything would be back the way it should be. Laura's goal had been achieved. Dover would carry on with its tradition intact.

He'd kept his promise to Laura and himself that he would complete his job. He'd wanted to prove to her that he could be counted on, that he could accomplish something important besides having a good time.

He turned his back, sensing a weight lift from his shoulders. He'd lost a lot this last month. His inheritance. Laura. But he'd also lost his self-centered attitude. His pride. His sense of entitlement. In its place he'd found his faith and the God he'd forgotten. He'd found compassion and the satisfaction of doing for others. It was time to go home and try once more to set things straight with his dad.

Adam picked up the nail gun and the few remaining cypress shingles on the scaffold. He reached for the rail and froze. A deep sense of dread filled his heart. Once he stepped off the scaffold, his time in Dover would be over. Officially, not until tomorrow morning, but in every way that mattered, it was over now.

He'd never see Laura again.

Adam signed his name and took a deep breath. It was done. He was a free man again. He slipped his wallet into his pocket, the familiar weight bringing a smile to his face. He scooped up the rest of his personal belongings and turned to face Tom Durrant. He'd been kind enough to bring him to the police station this morning to be processed.

Tom had a warm smile on his face. "Well, how does it feel? You can come and go as you please now."

"Great." He lifted his foot slightly. "And the lack of jewelry doesn't hurt either." He started to move, then remembered something important was missing from his stash. "My car keys."

Tom slipped his hand into his pocket and came up with the keys, dangling them in the air. "You looking for these?"

"How did you get them?"

"You'll see." He handed over the keys and placed a hand on Adam's shoulder, steering him to the door. "Be patient."

Adam's curiosity was spinning as they walked out of the police station. But the moment they approached the parking lot, the answer was waiting for him. Parked right in the first slot was his classic Porsche 356, sparkling clean and fully repaired. "My car." He hurried forward, inspecting the vehicle closely. "How did you manage this? I figured I'd have to rent something to get home. I asked about it several times, but no one would tell me anything."

"Well, don't thank me. I had a very small part in this."

Adam turned to face him, the sparkle in the man's eye speaking volumes. "Laura?" His tried to grasp the significance of her action. If she'd gone to all that trouble, then she must have some feelings for him. Something more than friendship and gratitude.

"She wanted you to know how grateful she was for all your help."

He looked around. "Where is she? I thought—"

"She's waiting at her house. She didn't want to see you here, like this."

Adam looked at the keys and then the car. He didn't understand.

Tom inclined his head. "Don't worry. She's anxious to see you. I promise. Adam, I don't know what the future may or may not hold for you and my daughter, but I want you to know that if you two decide to join your lives, I'd be proud to have you as a member of our family. You make my daughter happy and that's the most important thing to a father."

Tom's words of approval meant more than he could ever express. He shook his hand. "Thank you, sir. I'm deeply honored."

"Oh, I nearly forgot." Tom pulled an envelope from his jacket. "I picked this up on the way over here. I thought you might need it for today."

Adam took the envelope, unable to find words to express his appreciation. "Thank you for your help. I couldn't have pulled this off without you."

Tom waved off the gratitude. "Go. Talk to my girl."

The Dover town square was bustling with activity when Adam drove down Main Street a few minutes later. The scaffold had already been dismantled and painters were busy on the newly restored section of the gazebo. A delivery truck from a local garden center was being unloaded. Small tents and displays were going up all over the green for the arts and crafts vendors. Peace and Mill streets were already blocked off. In a few hours all evidence of his accident would be gone.

The light turned red and he stopped at the intersection. The same one where he'd lost control of his car and crashed into the gazebo. He eased off the gas, heading toward Laura's house, the nervous knot in his stomach growing. How would it feel standing in front of her as a free man? Not her saw boy. Not the prisoner in her father's home. But himself, the man who loved her?

But how did she feel? Could she love a man like him? Tom advised him to tell Laura how he felt, to let her decide. Shaw McKinney had reminded him that Laura deserved someone who could love her completely. So who did he listen to?

Chapter Eleven

Laura peeked out the dining room window, then moved to the front door to look at the street in front of her house. Wally barked and sat down in the middle of the hall. He'd been trailing at her heels all morning. Apparently he was tired of trying to keep up. Laura smiled and bent down to pet his head. "Sorry, fella. I just don't know what's taking him so long. He should have been here by now."

Adam was being released this morning. He was no longer a man confined by a sentence and an ankle monitor, and no longer someone she was responsible for. He was just Adam. Things would be different between them now and she couldn't wait to see him.

Her mother had convinced her that his attitude the other day had been from his need to finish the job and prove himself to her. She was hanging on to that hope. She would tell him how she felt and let God work it all out.

A flash of light flickered through the beveled glass door. "He's here." She hurried outside, waiting at the edge of the porch. She wanted to run to him and throw her arms around his neck, but their relationship hadn't progressed that far yet. She watched as he got out of the small car and came up the walk. He looked wonderful, but different. It was more than the dark jeans and the crisp blue cotton shirt he wore. More than the bronze jacket that made his green eyes fiery bright. There was a different tilt to his shoulders and a slow easy gait to his stride. Had freedom restored his confidence or was it something else?

He stopped at the foot of the porch steps. She searched his face for some clue to his emotions, finding herself captured by the warmth and affection in his green eyes. "Good morning."

He glanced toward his car. "You had it fixed."

"Were you surprised?" Her heart raced wildly in her chest.

"Shocked. How did you pull it off?"

"My dad helped. We sent it up to Jackson. There's a guy there who specializes in classic-car restoration."

He came up the steps, stopping in front of her. "Why did you do it?"

He was so close that she could feel his breath when he exhaled. She swayed against the attraction that washed over her. She opened her mouth to speak but her voice failed. She cleared her throat and tried again. "I knew how much it meant to you and I wanted to thank you for all your hard work. I'm only sorry that we couldn't get it done in time for you—"

Adam reached out and took her hand. "Don't. None of that matters." He touched the side of her face gently. "Laura, no one has ever done anything like that for me before."

"You deserved it. You worked hard and got the gazebo done on time. We're all so grateful to you." His eyes darkened to a forest green.

"Is that the only reason you did it? Out of gratitude?"

"No, I knew it would make you happy. And I want you to be happy."

Adam grasped her arms with his hands, drawing her ever closer. "Why?"

She held her breath, her eyes locked with his. She loved him. All she had to do was tell him. "Because… I care for you. A great deal."

Adam smiled. "How much do you care?" He lowered his head and kissed her lips lightly.

She melted into him, drowning in his tenderness.

"And I care about you, too, Laura."

She stepped back, needing to regain her senses. She tugged him toward the house. "Let's go inside. I want to talk."

He stopped abruptly, a teasing grin on his lips. "You going to present me with the repair bill?"

"No, silly." She pulled him along into the kitchen before releasing his hand. "I have coffee and muffins. Have a seat."

"Hey there, Wally." Adam tussled with the dog a moment before taking a seat at the table. She set the plate of muffins on the table along with a hot cup of coffee.

"Did you make these yourself?"

"Of course. My mother taught me and she's a very good cook." Adam smiled, making her heart skip again.

"I know. That's one of the things I'll miss about living there."

She started to ask him what else he would miss, but her courage failed her again. She started to move to the counter again, but Adam took her hand.

"I have something for you. I was going to wait and give it to you tomorrow, but I think this is the perfect time." He pulled a large envelope from his jacket and handed it to her.

Puzzled, she opened the flap and pulled out a legal document. "Oh." She read the paper twice, unable to believe what she was seeing. She looked at Adam for some explanation. "This is the deed to the Keller building."

He smiled. "Look at the bottom line."

Her eyes struggled to focus on the page. "It's in my name." She gasped, one hand covering her mouth in surprise. "How did you do this?"

"I made arrangements to buy it at the auction. I know how much it meant to you and I hated to see you lose it. Your dad helped me work out some of the details. He's a very influential man around here."

"My father?" She lowered the paper. "He's been a busy little fixer, hasn't he? Helping me with your car. Helping you with this." Tears clogged her throat and stung the back of her eyes. "Oh, Adam. I don't know what to say, how to thank you." She moved toward him, arms open. He stood and accepted her hug. She lifted her face to kiss him on the cheek, but he shifted, pulling her against him and capturing her mouth. She melted against him.

He ended the kiss, putting a little distance between them. "Lady, you're dangerous. I think we'd better get back to the muffins. You go sit over there and I'll sit here and we'll keep this nice table between us."

She smiled and nodded, exhaling a shaky breath. "Probably a wise move."

"So, tell me what you wanted to talk about."

"I want you to come to the festival tomorrow." She

chewed her lip, gathering her courage. "You deserve to participate and I want you to see how much having the gazebo done means to everyone."

"Is that the only reason?"

She shook her head, reaching out to gently touch his fingers. "I want to get to know you better. As a…friend, not an assignment."

"I want that, too, Laura."

"So you'll stay? You could even stay for Matt and Shelby's wedding if you'd like. It's next week."

"I'd like to, but I can't." He reached across the table and took her fingers in his. "I'll stay for the festival, but I can't stay any longer. I have to go back to Atlanta and talk to my father."

Her heart clenched. Maybe she'd read him wrong after all. "To see about your trust fund?"

"No. To try and reconcile with him. I've come to realize that I'm as much responsible for our bad relationship as he is. I've always blamed him for certain problems in my life, but I'm equally guilty. I have to try and work things out. Do you understand?"

She did, but she didn't like it. Glancing at the clock, her heart sank. She'd intended to talk to him about so many things and now she was out of time. "I need to leave in a few minutes. I'm driving up to Jackson today to meet with a potential client. Would you like to come along? We could have lunch. Talk."

"It's tempting, but I have some things to do before I leave. I'll pick you up tomorrow morning for the festival." He smiled. "That'll be a nice change. I'm looking forward to seeing you in my little car instead of your big truck."

Laura walked him to the door. He turned and pulled

her into his arms. "Laura…I…Thank you again for caring."

Laura rested her head against his chest, her arms around his waist. *Say it. Tell him now.* "You're welcome." She pulled back and looked up at him. "If you come early, we can have breakfast before we go."

"I'll call you when I get up." He bent and placed a kiss on her forehead.

"See you in the morning." She watched him go, wishing it was tomorrow, and wondering why she hadn't told him she loved him.

Laura stepped through the front door of her father's store, turning around to look at Adam. She wanted to see the expression on his face when he saw the town square for the first time. He strode out the door and froze. His eyes widened and his mouth fell open in stunned surprise. He moved to the curb, resting one hand on the iron poles supporting the balcony above the store. She went to his side, glancing back and forth between the scene on the square and the delight on his handsome face. "So? What do you think?"

Adam shook his head and looked at her, his green eyes bright. "This is wild. I had no idea, I expected a few booths and a food vendor or two. But this—" he reached over and pulled her to him "—this is totally unexpected."

Laura caught her breath. She was beginning to like that word. "Unexpected is good, right?"

"Very good."

She took his hand. "Come on. I want you to see everything." The sidewalk beside Durrant's was clogged with clothing racks and tables filled with jewelry and accessories from Jacqueline's Boutique next door, so they walked into the street. It was the only means of moving around the festival.

She'd hoped to have breakfast with Adam this morning, but he'd called last night and said he'd be tied up with some business matters in the morning. Waiting for him to pick her up had been nerve-racking, like waiting for Christmas morning to open her presents. Even the ride in his Porsche had been fun. They'd navigated the back streets and parked behind her dad's store. It was a good home base for the day and offered a respite from the noise and activity.

"Where did all these people come from? I didn't know Dover had this many people."

"Oh, our festival is a really big deal around here. We have hundreds of craft and food vendors from all over the country who are regulars. Some come from as far away as Canada and Mexico." Adam pulled out his phone and took a picture of the area.

Laura took a moment to survey her beloved town. The park around the courthouse was littered with white shade canopies all sheltering various crafts and specialty artists. The broad downtown streets, lined with food vendors in wagons, vans and tents, resembled the midway of a county fair. At the far end of the park stood the gazebo. She couldn't wait to take Adam there.

"This is crazy." Adam smiled down at her.

At the end of the block, Laura pointed down the side street. "The carnival rides are set up down there in an old grocery store parking lot. There's the usual stuff— Octopus, Tilt-a-Whirl, Ferris wheel. If you're looking for a thrill, we could head that direction."

Adam squeezed her hand. "You're thrilling enough."

Her heart melted. "That's also the street where the parade will be."

"A parade? Through all this activity?"

'No. The children's parade. It starts at the old church a couple blocks down and ends right before this intersection. Kenny and Chester will be in it, so we don't want to miss that."

Adam frowned. "Chester? Have I missed a nephew somewhere?"

"No, silly. Chester is his dog. The kids and pets dress alike. It's always fun." Laura continued the tour, strolling along Peace Street and crossing onto Main Street. "The stage is on the far corner. You'll hear all kinds of music throughout the day. Gospel. Rock. Country. The local talent winners will be singing this morning, and tonight we have a famous country group coming in."

"Hey, Mr. Holbrook."

Laura looked around as a man about her father's age approached. She felt Adam brace and gently touched his side.

The man extended his hand, a friendly smile on his face. "My name's Elliot, Ben Elliot. I just wanted to thank you for working so hard to get that gazebo up and ready for this weekend. I live in Sawyers Bend and I know the gazebo belongs to Dover, but we have a special attachment to that little building, too."

Adam cleared his throat and took the man's hand. "Thank you. I appreciate that."

Mr. Elliot nodded, smiled at Laura, then moved off.

"That was a first."

"What do you mean?"

"No one has ever appreciated anything I did."

"I appreciate you." She slipped her arm in his and

started walking again. "Okay, your tour is over. Time
to get down to some serious exploration. First we'll
shop, then we'll eat. Then shop some more and then
eat more." She grinned up at him. "Any objections?"

"I just do what I'm told, boss."

Laura took his hand, entwining her fingers with his
and wishing she could keep him at her side always.

Adam leaned against the trunk of the old magnolia
tree beside the gazebo. The same one he and Jim had
met under. Laura had taken her numerous packages
to her father's store, giving Adam the first chance to
catch his breath. She'd been like a kid in a candy shop
all morning, scurrying from one attraction to another.
He'd happily followed along, marveling at her energy
and her joy. He'd be perfectly content to bask in the
glow of her delight for the rest of his life.

His gaze drifted toward the gazebo. His reason for
being here. People wandered in and around the structure. Some had taken the steps into the center, sitting
and talking for a while. Others had stopped and taken
pictures. Small groups of kids had raced in and around
and down the steps again in a game of tag. One couple had slipped inside for a kiss. Hardly a moment had
passed when the beloved landmark went unused.

Laura had wanted to make it their first stop this
morning, but somehow they'd been redirected to talk
to friends or family, then lunch with the Durrants.
He'd been convinced to try chicken on a stick and fried
Twinkies. His stomach would never be the same.

He glanced back toward Durrant's Hardware. He'd
learned a lot about Laura today. She liked handmade
jewelry and paintings of gardens. Her taste in scarves

leaned toward vibrant colors. She bought any kind of handmade soap, and she had a weakness for funnel cakes. He smiled thinking of her excitement. Laura found something beautiful in everything her eyes touched. From wind chimes to rusty old tools. He couldn't even count the number of times they'd stopped to greet friends and acquaintances, a couple of whom Adam had helped through the Handy Works ministry.

They'd watched the children's parade, cheering for Kenny and his dog, who were dressed like Insect Man. He had no idea who or what that was, but it was the cutest thing he'd ever seen.

This afternoon Laura had promised to take Kenny to the Kids' Zone. From what he could gather, there would be face painting, balloon animals and an inflatable jump house. Cassidy had convinced her aunt to go with her to the Dover princess pageant, claiming she needed to observe for when she was sixteen and could participate.

A month ago Adam would have called all this the worst kind of corny, but now he wanted to soak it all in. The music, the sights, the delectable smells all gave him a sense of belonging. Of home.

"Adam."

He turned, coming face-to-face with Shaw McKinney. He braced. Had he come to warn him away from Laura again? "Shaw."

McKinney smiled and extended his hand. "Good to see you here."

Adam nodded, sensing there was more to come.

"I wanted to let you know I've changed my mind about some things." He slipped his hands into the back pockets of his jeans and inhaled a slow, measured breath. "You did a good job on the gazebo. Better than

I expected. And you worked hard to get it done. That means a lot. Mostly, I wanted to tell you that I was wrong about you and LC. Forget what I said. You're a good man."

Stunned, Adam took a moment to find his voice. "Thanks, but I don't think I understand."

Shaw smiled and punched him lightly on the shoulder. "I saw for myself how much you love her, man. That's all that matters."

"Shaw, sweetie, I got your drink."

A fiery redhead in skinny jeans and a flouncy top sidled up to Shaw and smiled. "Thanks. Tell LC I said hello. You planning on staying in Dover, Adam?"

"I don't know yet."

"Well, if you do, you'd be a welcome addition."

Speechless, Adam watched the couple walk away.

"Was that Shaw?" Laura appeared at his side.

Adam nodded. "He said to say hello. I think that's the first time I've seen him smile. He was always so sour when we worked together."

"Are you kidding? Shaw is as easygoing as they come. And the most eligible bachelor in Dover. I doubt if there's a woman alive who could get him to settle down."

A slow smiled moved his lips. "That's what they used to say about me, too."

Laura blushed and took his hand, glancing at the gazebo. "So what do you think?"

Arm in arm they strolled slowly toward the cherished landmark, an odd mixture of pride and affection swirling in Adam's chest. The gazebo had been completely transformed. All signs of construction had vanished. The once-trampled and muddy ground around the site was now covered with thick, lush sod. Small shrubs and colorful flowers encircled the foundation like a living wreath. A necklace of bunting in green and gold draped around the lattice inserts at the roofline and wrapped around the thick turned posts.

They stopped at the base of the steps. Laura squeezed his arm.

"What do you think?"

"It looks like it's never been touched." He gazed down at her. "You do amazing work."

"You helped. I couldn't have done it without you."

Laura started up the steps, the ones he'd help build. Inside the gazebo, Adam made a slow tour of the structure. He ran a hand along the handrail and over one of the posts, remembering the work he'd put into it. A swell of pride expanded his chest. The accomplishment was a turning point in his life. He understood now the importance of the landmark and what it meant to Dover.

Laura slipped her arm around his waist. "You're a part of us now, Adam. Every time you think of Dover, you'll remember the work you put into this gazebo. You'll carry us with you wherever you go and we'll always have a part of you here with us."

With a fresh coat of paint covering the entire gazebo, he could almost believe nothing had happened. But a great deal had happened. This little building had changed his life. He turned to face Laura, looking deep into her eyes, watching them turn deep purple. Was she remembering the kiss that day in the rain? He started to pull her closer only to remember there were no tarps to shield them today.

He took her hand and started toward the steps. He wished he could capture this moment. Pulling his phone from his pocket, he turned on the camera, flagging down a passerby to take their picture in the gazebo. He pulled Laura to his side, gazing down at her, knowing in his very depths that he belonged at her side. If only he had the courage to tell her how he felt.

Laura gazed out over the courthouse square now bathed in the warmth of streetlights and strings of twinkle lights. The gazebo lights had blinked on, casting a romantic curtain of light down along its sides. From the balcony of her father's store she had a panoramic view of the downtown. Music from the stage across the square floated on the air, underscored by the tinny sound of the carnival rides a few blocks over. The white canopies over the vendors glowed in the waning daylight. She inhaled a deep breath, smiling at the tantalizing aromas of the carnival foods available below.

She smiled when Adam join her, laying his hand over hers on the rail. "This is one of my favorite days of the year. I love the festival."

"I think it's become one of mine, too."

They watched in companionable silence a moment. "We have one more thing to do." She turned and looked at him. "The balloon glow."

"Don't think I've ever been to one."

"What? A world traveler like you?"

"I'm beginning to see my world was missing some key stops. When and where do we view this spectacular sight?"

She pointed toward the southwest side of town. "There's an open field where the balloons are set up. Once it's dark they'll fire up the burners and inflate the balloons. I heard there are going be nearly two dozen this year. It's my favorite part."

Adam slipped an arm around her waist. "I think every part of the festival is your favorite."

Laura giggled. "Guess so."

They caught the tractor-pulled shuttle at the edge of the square and took the bumpy ride to the field. Adam took her hand as they followed the crowds gathering for the event. "I know a good spot to watch from. It's a longer walk, but it'll be worth it." She took a path away from the crowds and up a slight slope. When they reached a rustic wooden fence, she bent down and slipped between the rails. Adam raised an eyebrow. "It's all right. This is part of Uncle Hank's land."

She stopped beneath a live oak, pointing toward the field. "You can see all the balloons from up here."

Adam took her hand in his, pulling her against his side. "I can see all I want to right here."

Now was her chance, the opportunity she'd waited for all day. She'd tell him how she felt, ask him to stay. "Adam, I want to talk to you about something."

"All right. As long as it's nothing bad. I don't want anything to spoil this day. I want to concentrate on you and make each moment count." He held her gaze a moment then glanced off toward the field. "I think your glow is starting."

She turned, finding herself in the circle of his arms, her back resting against his chest.

In the field below, the balloons started to billow and move as the propane burners coughed hot air inside them. The flames from the burners flashed in spurts of gold like fireflies.

First one, then another slowly inflated, their large envelopes coming to life. Some were a solid color, some multicolored stripes, others carried company logos. A few were in whimsical shapes. A house. An animal. Even an oddly shaped balloon tree. The field suddenly exploded in glowing color.

Within minutes the balloons were upright, tethered to the ground, but their expanded envelopes rising like glowing mushrooms side by side across the field. "Isn't it beautiful?"

Adam wrapped his arm tighter around her. "It is, but not as beautiful as you."

"Tomorrow morning they'll all take to the air and float over Dover. I love waking up to the sound of the burners. They drift on the wind so silent and beautiful. I think riding in one might be a small adventure I'd like to try someday."

"I'll see what I can do."

Laura closed her eyes, imprinting this day in her memory. A perfect day. A perfect man. Now was the time to say the words. "Adam…"

A jarring blast of sound broke into the quiet. Adam pulled his phone from his pocket and turned away. She heard him mutter under his breath, then groan. "What is it?" The look on his face scared her. "Adam, what's wrong?"

"It's my father. He's suffered a heart attack. He's in critical condition. I have to go, Laura. I need to be there."

Her disappointment was quickly replace with concern. "Of course you do. We'll head back right now." She pulled her own phone from her pocket and touched her travel app. "I'll see if I can get you a flight out of Jackson to Atlanta tonight. It's the closest airport, but there aren't many flights. If we can't get a flight out of there, we'll try New Orleans, but it's a two-hour drive from here." Adam took her arm, guiding her through the fence and back down the hill. The shuttle returned them to the square. Back in her father's house, Adam stopped and placed his hands on her arms.

"I wanted to talk to you. I had so much to say, but now…"

She shook her head. "It's all right. We'll talk when you come back. You will come back, won't you?" He hesitated before replying, sending her heart into a deep chill.

"I'll try." He kissed her forehead, then hurried upstairs to pack. Twenty minutes later he was gone, leaving her alone and with a mountain of doubt weighing down her heart.

Chapter Twelve

The antiseptic smell permeated everywhere, even the elevator. Adam doubted he'd ever get used to it. The doors slid open and he stepped out onto the fifth floor of Hillside Hospital, heading toward his father's room. The sight of Orson Gould standing outside filled him with a surge of alarm. He quickened his steps. "Orson, what's happened?"

The slender man, his father's longtime legal counsel and close friend, held up his hand. "He's fine. In fact, it's good news for a change."

Adam released a heartfelt sigh, resting his hands on his hips. In the weeks since he'd come home, his father had suffered another heart attack and major surgery. It would be nice to get some encouraging news for a change.

"I spoke with his physician a few minutes ago, and they believe he'll be able to go home in a few days. I'm going to start making arrangements for his care. Will you be staying on?"

"No. If he's improved that much, there's no reason for me to stay in Atlanta."

Orson stared at him a moment. "Adam, I want you to know, I tried my best to get him to change his mind about the will and the trust fund, but he's stubborn. Once he makes up his mind…"

"I know." He patted the man's shoulder. Orson was his only contact to his father, the only one he could call for help. "I appreciate it."

"Perhaps now that he's had this brush with death, he'll be more amenable to change, at least to restoring your trust fund."

Adam shook his head. "I don't care about the money, Orson. I've found something better."

"Better?"

"I've found peace. And hopefully a home."

Orson nodded. "Ah. You're referring to that matter I helped you with recently in Duncan, Mississippi?"

"Dover. Yes."

"Well, I sincerely hope it works out. I'll talk to you later."

Adam stood outside the room for a moment, praying for another dose of patience and understanding. So far his visits to his father had all started and ended the same way. A less-than-welcome greeting and an order to stay away. He pushed the door open.

His father was sitting in the chair today, a vast improvement. "Hello, Dad. It's good to see you out of that bed. How are you feeling?"

He cursed and glared. "You back again? I don't need you here."

Adam swallowed the knot of hurt and moved to the chair beside his father. "They tell me you're going home soon."

"What's it to you?"

"I'm concerned."

"Concerned about your money. I told you, you're not getting it back."

"I'm not here for the money, Dad. I'm here for you. For us."

"What's that supposed to mean?"

They'd been down this same road before. Adam rubbed the bridge of his nose in frustration. Maybe it was time to lay things on the line. "I came to ask your forgiveness, Dad. I know I haven't been the son you wanted and I'm sorry. I'm hoping you'll forgive me."

Arthur Holbrook jerked his head around. "If this is some of that religious junk you're trying on me, I won't have it."

"No, Dad. I just don't want us to be angry at each other anymore. I'm accepting my part in our strained relationship and I've forgiven you for yours."

"Forgive me. For what?"

"Not being there. Not being a father when I needed it."

"I gave you everything you needed. You threw it all away on fool stunts. Without my money you'll be nothing."

Adam stood. There was no point in continuing. He'd done what he'd come to do. "You're wrong. I've found everything. My faith, a home and someone I want to spend my life with."

"She only wants your money. Once she knows you're penniless she'll leave."

"She already knows and it doesn't make any difference." He walked to the door, all hope of reconciling gone. "I'm going back to her as soon as I can make arrangements. Goodbye, Dad. Take care of yourself."

He had one foot in the corridor when he heard his father call his name.

"You ever coming home again?"

He turned to face his father, surprised to find the stern features had softened a bit, and a faint pleading in his dark eyes. A grain of hope, smaller than a mustard seed, sprouted in Adam's heart. "I'd like you to meet her. Her name is Laura and I think you'd like her."

Arthur Holbrook turned his head. "Suit yourself."

It wasn't much, but it was something. Adam strode down the corridor. He'd done all he could. Now it was time to return to Dover and talk to Laura. He just prayed he hadn't stayed away too long.

On Thanksgiving Day, Laura slipped away from the kitchen and sought out the quiet of the formal living room in her parents' home, tucking herself into the corner of the sofa. Normally this was one of her most cherished family holidays. Having her family gathered around, talking, laughing, sharing a turkey dinner filled her heart to overflowing. But this year something, no, *someone,* was missing, and it was hard to enjoy the day not knowing where he was or what he was doing. More important, why hadn't he contacted her since leaving Dover?

Laura fingered her cell phone a moment, then pulled up her contact list. She paused with her finger on the call key. All she had to do was touch it and wait for him to answer. She could say she wanted to know how his father was. It was the truth, but not as much as she wanted to know about him.

The only message she'd received was the photo he'd sent of them taken in the gazebo at the festival. He'd captioned it with the words *Perfect Day*. She'd examined the photo dozens of times, looking for some reassurance in his smile, his eyes. One time she'd thought she saw love in his green eyes. But the next time she didn't see anything but a man having a nice day with a friend.

Closing her eyes, she let her hand fall to her lap, her conflicted emotions immobilizing her once again. She'd tried to call him several times in the last three weeks, but her courage had always failed at the last moment. What was the point, after all? Eventually she'd had to face the truth. Once he'd returned to his life in Atlanta, he'd realized the differences between them were too great.

"Why won't you call him?"

Laura opened her eyes. Her new sister-in-law, Shelby Russell, no, Durrant, was frowning at her. "What good would it do?"

"Maybe none. Maybe a lot. But you won't know until you try."

She shook her head. "It's all my fault. I was asking him to be something he wasn't. I misread everything." She drew her knees up under her so Shelby could join her on the sofa. "What's that old saying? You can take the man out of the city, but you can't take the city out of the man?"

"I don't think that's the way I've heard it, but I get your point." She rested a hand on Laura's. "You miss him, don't you?"

Laura blinked as tears stung her eyes. "Only every time I see that stupid gazebo. I dialed his number once, at your and Matt's reception."

"But you didn't wait for him to answer, did you?"

"No, I chickened out. I thought he cared, but it's been weeks now without a call. All he's sent is one stupid picture."

"What picture?"

Laura pulled it up on her phone and handed it to Shelby.

"Uh, Laura, honey, that is a picture of a man crazy in love."

She took the phone back. "A man in love calls. How lame is that? I believed him when he said, 'I'll call you.' There's only one way to interpret that, Shelby. He's moved on."

Shelby exhaled a grunt of frustration. "Laura, the man bought you a building. I'd say that was a pretty good clue that he loves you."

Laura nodded in agreement. "That was very sweet."

"You really don't know what he's dealing with right now. He's probably tied up at the hospital with his father. You said he was in critical condition."

She drew her legs all the way to her chest and laid her head on her knees. "I know. And I feel awful for focusing on me and not him. I've prayed that his father will be all right and they can find a way to reconcile, but it would help if I knew what was going on."

"I know. But I'd be willing to guess that he's been so tied up with his father he just hasn't had time to call."

"Or it could be that I'm a really lousy judge of men."

"If you mean to say Adam wasn't worth your affection, then yes, you are."

"You didn't know him like I did."

"Maybe not, but your parents and your brother thought well of him and I trust their judgment."

Laura glanced over her shoulder. "Right. Like Dad

showed good judgment when he put the store up for sale?"

"None of you guys wanted it, and he and your mom are ready to retire and enjoy themselves."

"I know, it's just too much to process at once. Matt and you getting married, Dad selling the store, Adam leaving town."

"Call him, Laura. It's Thanksgiving. You have the perfect excuse."

Laura gave her sister-in-law a hug. "Thanks. I'll think about it."

She stared at her phone again, her courage waning. This is what happened when she lacked faith. Her fear of being hurt again had prevented her from telling Adam she loved him. Now he was gone and she wouldn't have the chance to.

She rose and started back toward the kitchen, banishing thoughts of Adam to the far recesses of her mind. Today was all about family. She should focus on that.

Sounds of a football game on the television carried throughout the house. Laughter from the kitchen bounced off the walls, interspersed with the shouts and giggles of her niece and nephew. The noise and commotion that normally comforted her now left her feeling alone and sad.

Pulling a large clip from her backpack, she secured her hair on top of her head, then grabbed her jacket from the hall closet. She had time for a walk before dinner was ready. Fresh air and open space might be what she needed to get herself under control.

Adam stood on the sidewalk outside the Durrant home, gearing up the courage to knock on the door. It was Thanksgiving Day. He hadn't realized it until he'd boarded the plane this morning. Not only was he intruding into Laura's life again, but he was doing it on a major family holiday. He slipped his hands into his jacket pockets and stared at the house again, leaning against the tree trunk at the curb.

He could see them moving around in the dining room at the front of the house. He shouldn't be staring in their windows like a Peeping Tom, but he was compelled to watch them. What he really was longing for was a glimpse of Laura. He wanted to talk to her alone, not with the entire Durrant clan hovering around

Coward. Truth was, he was nervous about seeing her again. He hadn't called her once since he'd left Dover. Not the way a man trying to win the woman he loved should behave. He'd lost big points there. He knew he'd be welcome in the Durrants' home, but it wasn't their welcome he sought. He'd screwed up and he'd prayed all the way from Atlanta that it wasn't too late, that Laura hadn't forgotten him and moved on.

He should have taken her father's advice. If he would have told Laura how he felt the day he'd given her the deed to the Keller building, they could have worked through the separation together. Instead, he'd chickened out, afraid of not measuring up to the man she idolized—her father. Now he was afraid he might have lost his chance with her forever.

He prayed he'd made the right choice. He'd made a major life decision on faith, trusting that the Lord would actually work this one out. Something he'd never done before.

A noise drew his attention to the front door of the Durrants' two-story colonial. Someone stepped out and hurried down the porch steps and onto the sidewalk along the street. His heart flipped over in his chest a couple of times. Laura. She was a vision in black jeans, heeled boots and a lavender sweater that matched her eyes. He straightened and stepped toward her.

"Adam!"

The sweet, lilting tone of her voice washed over him. She looked soft and beautiful, exactly the way he'd remembered her. Even with her silken hair pulled up into that ridiculous bun on the top of her head. The look in her eyes sent his heart pounding. Was she happy to see him?

"Hi." He wanted to memorize every inch of her. He might not get another chance. The smile on her face gave him hope.

"You came back?" She moved to him, resting her hands on his chest. He took her shoulders in his hands.

"I had to. I missed you."

"I missed you, too."

Suddenly he felt like an awkward, insecure kid. Where did he start? How did he tell her what was in his heart? He saw his own uncertainty reflected in her violet eyes.

"How's your father?"

"Better. It was touch and go for a while, but the doctors think he'll make a full recovery." Nerves and anxiety churned in his stomach. He needed to move before he jumped out of his skin. "Let's walk. We have a lot to talk about." She fell into step beside him as they strolled down the block, slipping her hand through the crook of his arm.

"Did you work things out between you?"

"Let's just say it's a work in progress and that I have hope. I'd like to take you to meet him."

"I'd like that."

"I'm sorry I didn't call. I was tied up at the hospital with my dad around the clock in the beginning. When things finally settled down, so much time had passed I wasn't sure how you'd feel. I sent the picture so you wouldn't forget me."

"I could never forget you. That was a perfect day for me, too."

Adam stopped and pulled Laura around to face him. "A very wise man gave me some advice and I didn't take it. I regret that more than I can say. So I'm taking it now." He inhaled and gazed into her eyes. "Laura, I love you. I want to spend the rest of my life with you."

The smile on her face sent his heart soaring.

"You love me? Oh, Adam, I love you, too. I wanted to tell you that night at the balloon glow, but I was so afraid you didn't feel the same way. You told me you could never survive in a place like Dover."

"I know, but that was before a beautiful lady carpenter stole my heart. I think I fell in love with the you the first time I saw you." He reached up and pulled the clips from her hair.

"And I've loved you from the moment I saw you standing in my brother's old room, wearing that tattered tuxedo and that bandage on your chin."

Adam laughed and pulled her into his arms. "So will you marry me, Laura?"

"Yes!"

She threw her arms around his neck and kissed him, dispelling any and all doubts. Breathless, he pulled back, cradling her face in his hands. "I thought about bringing a ring with me, but I want you to pick out the exact one you want. I'd like that to be the first thing we do together as a couple." He searched her eyes for confirmation.

Laura's eyes filled with tears, her fingers pressed against her lips. Had he already messed up?

"Oh, Adam, how did you know? Did you talk to my dad?"

He shook his head. "No, I never mentioned it."

"You're just like my dad. The first thing he and Mom did when they decided to get married was choose the ring together. I've always thought that was so romantic. The perfect way to start a life together.

She hugged him again. "I told you if I ever found someone as wonderful as my father, I'd marry him." She smiled into his eyes, her small hand on his cheek.

They'd reached the end of the block and started back. "Do you think your parents will be happy?"

"Totally. Mom has been singing your praises since the beginning. You're not going back to Atlanta now, are you? You're staying in Dover?"

"I'm staying." That earned him another hug.

"What will you do? You'll have to find a job. I can put you on as one of my crew or you could run Handy Works."

"Actually, I have something else in mind. In fact, it's already in the works. I was only waiting to see if I was still welcome in your life before completing the details."

"What?"

"I happen to know a man who is very interested in buying your dad's store. Keeping it in the family, so to speak." He watched as she processed what he'd said.

"Who? You? Oh, that's the perfect solution!"

Side by side they started up toward her parents' front porch.

"So when do you want to make this official?"

Laura squeezed his arm. "How about Valentine's Day?"

He nodded. Not too far off but plenty of time for her to plan the kind of wedding she would want. "You should be able to have your passport by then."

"Why do I need one?"

"You can't spend a honeymoon in England without one."

"Adam Holbrook, I love you." They stopped at the foot of the porch steps.

Adam started to kiss her again when the front door opened and Angie Durrant appeared.

"Laura? Adam! Oh, how wonderful. Tom! Adam is here."

Tom joined his wife at the door. "Hey, Adam. I thought you might turn up today. What are you two doing out there? Dinner is almost ready. It's Thanksgiving, remember?"

Laura slipped her arm around Adam. "Dad. Mom. There's something we need to tell you."

Her mother waved her off. "We know. Come on inside."

Tom waited for Adam, laying a fatherly arm across his shoulders. "Come on, son. We can't start Thanksgiving unless the whole family is here."

* * * * *

Dear Reader,

I hope you enjoyed Adam and Laura's story and your second trip to Dover, Mississippi. I'm always amazed and delighted when the Lord gives us detours. At the time, they make us upset and irritated because our plans have been disturbed. We've all had them, myself included. But on the other side of the detour, life can hold some surprises and blessings we never imagined. It's during these times we must hold on and trust the Lord to work it all out for good. Adam had a lot to lose when he landed in jail, but what he found during his journey made it all worthwhile.

This story was inspired by a song about a man who had experienced every wild adventure on the planet, but he'd never experienced anything like the emotions he felt when he fell in love. I wanted to take Adam from a man who was looking for adventure in outside things to a man who found love and adventure in caring for others and for someone special. As a result, Adam had blessings heaped upon him that he never could have envisioned. A good lesson for all of us to remember. With the Lord's help, we can all change and become more than we think we are.

I love to hear from readers. You can visit me at LorraineBeatty.blogspot.com.

Lorraine Beatty

Questions for Discussion

1. Laura makes a snap judgment about Adam from his reputation. She learns that her perceptions were wrong. What do we lose when we make quick assessments about others without getting to know them first?

2. Adam comes to see that the problems between him and his father are partly his fault. Discuss why it is so hard for us to admit being at fault and then seek forgiveness.

3. Both Adam and Laura received good advice on how to proceed in their relationship, but neither one followed it. How do you decide if advice you've received is worth considering? Talk about what the Bible says about seeking wide counsel.

4. Adam has his worldly life reduced to a very small area—the Durrants' house and the gazebo. What did he learn by looking at things more closely, without the distraction of the next adventure?

5. Adam gave his heart to the Lord as a young man, but without someone to guide and teach him, he drifted away from his faith. Have you known someone who drifted or have you drifted because you lacked guidance? How can you make sure you're connected to your faith?

6. Laura loved her job, but she allowed her mistakes from the past to keep her from reaching for love

again. What should she have done with her pain instead of holding on to it? Why do you think she didn't do that?

7. Adam is desperate to get home in time to meet his financial deadline, but staying in Dover revealed to him a different path to his future. Has the Lord ever placed you in a difficult spot that in the end proved to be a much better way?

8. Forgiveness is one of the hardest things God asks us to do. Adam may never get his father's forgiveness, but he forgave his father for his neglect. How do you think that changed Adam? What benefit did he get from forgiving his father?

9. Adam and Laura had opposite views of life. He liked the unexpected. She liked the predictable. How did they learn to appreciate each other's differences?

10. Adam was uncomfortable and insecure in the Durrants' family gatherings because he had no experience with it. Did the Durrants' do enough to make him feel at home or could they have done more?

11. It seemed like everything was working against Laura and Adam as they tried to finish the gazebo on time, but the Lord worked it all out in the end. It never feels like it will work out when we are in the middle of difficult time. Talk about some of those times and share how you dealt with it.

12. Laura was surprised when Adam performed a self-
    less act, not realizing that she had been his role
    model. Discuss how we must be aware of the things
    we do and say, because they are Christ's represen-
    tatives in all we do.

COMING NEXT MONTH from Love Inspired®
AVAILABLE JUNE 18, 2013

LOVE IN BLOOM
The Heart of Main Street
Arlene James
With the help of handsome widowed rancher Tate Bronson and his little girl-turned-matchmaker, can Lily Farnsworth create a garden of community and love deep in the heart of Kansas...and one special man?

BABY IN HIS ARMS
Whisper Falls
Linda Goodnight
When helicopter pilot Creed Carter finds an abandoned baby on a church altar, he must convince foster parent Haley Blanchard that she'll make a good mom—and a good match.

NOAH'S SWEETHEART
Lancaster County Weddings
Rebecca Kertz
Noah Lapp captures Rachel Hostetler's heart from the moment he rescues her from a runaway buggy, but he's expected to marry Rachel's cousin. Too bad the heart doesn't always follow plans....

MONTANA WRANGLER
Charlotte Carter
When Paige Barclay suddenly becomes guardian to her nephew, she finds herself clashing with ranch foreman Jay Red Elk over what's best for the boy. Will these stubborn hearts ever fall in love?

SMALL-TOWN MOM
Jean C. Gordon
Nurse Jamie Glasser has managed to shut all things military out of her life. But former army captain Eli Payton can help her troubled son—if Jamie will let him in.

HIS UNEXPECTED FAMILY
Patricia Johns
As police chief, Greg Taylor has the task of delivering an orphaned infant to the care of Emily Shaw. He never expected to become wrapped around this baby's heart—or her mother's.

Look for these and other Love Inspired books wherever books are sold, including most bookstores, supermarkets, discount stores and drugstores.

LICNM0613

REQUEST YOUR FREE BOOKS!

2 FREE INSPIRATIONAL NOVELS
PLUS 2
FREE
MYSTERY GIFTS

Love Inspired®

YES! Please send me 2 FREE Love Inspired® novels and my 2 FREE mystery gifts (gifts are worth about $10). After receiving them, if I don't wish to receive any more books, I can return the shipping statement marked "cancel." If I don't cancel, I will receive 6 brand-new novels every month and be billed just $4.74 per book in the U.S. or $5.24 per book in Canada. That's a saving of at least 21% off the cover price. It's quite a bargain! Shipping and handling is just 50¢ per book in the U.S. and 75¢ per book in Canada.* I understand that accepting the 2 free books and gifts places me under no obligation to buy anything. I can always return a shipment and cancel at any time. Even if I never buy another book, the two free books and gifts are mine to keep forever.   105/305 IDN F47Y

Name _____ (PLEASE PRINT) _____

Address _____ Apt. # _____

City _____ State/Prov. _____ Zip/Postal Code _____

Signature (if under 18, a parent or guardian must sign) _____

Mail to the Harlequin® Reader Service:
IN U.S.A.: P.O. Box 1867, Buffalo, NY 14240-1867
IN CANADA: P.O. Box 609, Fort Erie, Ontario L2A 5X3

**Are you a subscriber to Love Inspired books
and want to receive the larger-print edition?
Call 1-800-873-8635 or visit www.ReaderService.com.**

* Terms and prices subject to change without notice. Prices do not include applicable taxes. Sales tax applicable in N.Y. Canadian residents will be charged applicable taxes. Offer not valid in Quebec. This offer is limited to one order per household. Not valid for current subscribers to Love Inspired books. All orders subject to credit approval. Credit or debit balances in a customer's account(s) may be offset by any other outstanding balance owed by or to the customer. Please allow 4 to 6 weeks for delivery. Offer available while quantities last.

Your Privacy—The Harlequin® Reader Service is committed to protecting your privacy. Our Privacy Policy is available online at www.ReaderService.com or upon request from the Harlequin Reader Service.

We make a portion of our mailing list available to reputable third parties that offer products we believe may interest you. If you prefer that we not exchange your name with third parties, or if you wish to clarify or modify your communication preferences, please visit us at www.ReaderService.com/consumerschoice or write to us at Harlequin Reader Service Preference Service, P.O. Box 9062, Buffalo, NY 14269. Include your complete name and address.

SADDLE UP AND READ 'EM!

This summer, get your fix of Western reads and pick up a cowboy from the INSPIRATIONAL category in July!

THE OUTLAW'S REDEMPTION
by Renee Ryan
from Love Inspired Historical

MONTANA WRANGLER
by Charlotte Carter
from Love Inspired

*Look for these great Western reads AND MORE,
available wherever books are sold or visit*
www.Harlequin.com/Westerns